For my beautiful wife
Sara

With thanks to all
friends and colleagues who have
contributed to this book

Illustrations by

Pad Lhula Lon

a very quiet, unassuming Vietnamese boy,
who not once appears in the pages you are about to read,
neither in the punishment records, nor for receiving any merits
or prizes; instead, he was all the time drawing and sketching
the characters and places in St. Cretien's College

ST. CRETIEN'S COLLEGE

An independent co-ed boarding school

for pupils aged 11-18 years

TEACHER OF MODERN LANGUAGES

To start from September 2009

This post would suit an enthusiastic, well-qualified teacher of French and/or Russian/German, including NQT's.

Set in beautiful grounds, the school offers an all-round education to all manner of children, not just those of the affluent or nouveau-riche

**Applications to be sent to the Head Master
via the School Office by February Friday 13th, 2009**

www.stcretiens.org.uk

St. Cretien's College is a registered charity No. 9834-59078582-3409555833

19 Semmingbury Way,
Canonsborough,
Herefordshire

Weds. 21st January, 2009

The Head Master,
St. Cretien's School,
West Sussex

Dear Mr. Warble,

I would like to apply for the post of French teacher at St. Cretien's College, as advertised in the latest edition of *The *** Supplement*.

Although it might appear from my enclosed CV that I am somewhat inexperienced in the whole field of teaching within the independent boarding sector, I do feel that I have enough expertise working in languages and with young people, coupled with plenty of energy and enthusiasm, for me to fit in well to this position. I should admit, now, that I am not particularly fond of working with children, and that the work I have done on occasions with local groups was, according to my referees, effectively done, in spite of the fact that I did not derive a great deal of fulfilment from the experiences.

I am, however, very keen to work within the stimulating and dynamic environment of a school. Over recent months, as you will see from my CV, I have worked in a telephone-sales office, trying to promote stalls at a refuse/recycling fair to foreign companies, but I did not find this a particularly rewarding way of working with my knowledge of languages. I have also had a number of unfortunate incidents when doing work-experience with a translation firm, resulting in difficult and complex law-suits; incidentally, please do not try to contact this particular previous employer, as they are no longer trading under the same name as on my CV.

As well as an active interest in languages and travelling, I have a real passion for meteorological patterns, and have presented talks to my local *Weathermen Society* and *Cloudwatchers Club*, the latter of which made me Secretary General in August 2008. Being able to discern long-term weather patterns is something I would like to apply to my teaching in some way, though I am not yet sure how this might actually happen. It may be that there is the chance of setting up a club or lunchtime society within the school, where my knowledge of weather patterns could be used.

I might also add that I am an avid enthusiast of hinges, and have amassed a collection of just over 20,000.

I look forward to hearing further from you.
Yours sincerely,

Henry Pukeman

The Master's Lodge,
Sedgwickham,
West Sussex,

20th February, 2009

Dear Mr. Pukeman,
Thank-you again for attending the interview last week. I am delighted to be able to confirm in writing your appointment as Teacher of French at St Cretien's College, to begin in September 2009. We were very impressed by your candid approach to the interviews, and felt you would bring a great deal of youthful enthusiasm to the school.

I do hope that you will accept our offer, and I would also like to extend my own personal welcome to you. I am sure, too, that you will find St. Cretien's a most welcoming place both to live and to work in, and I do hope you will settle quickly into life here. As we say here at St. Cretien's, "A new friend within the nest is doubly a friend amongst friends without a nest." I feel that says a great deal about how you will find your time here at St. Cretien's; in fact, it must be said that a good number of staff arrive and find the place very agreeable indeed, and stay much longer than they expected; most only ever leave in a box!

In fact, your arrival in September will coïncide with a remarkable term in the school's history, as we will be celebrating St. Cretien's 150th anniversary in some style! This sesquicentennial year since the school's foundation is likely to be one to remember, let me assure you, as the whole place will be putting on quite a show, from the pupils through to the staff. Alongside all the pomp taking place within the school, there is also to be a solemn parade through the local town of Sedgwickham, in order to unveil a small memorial to where the school started out, before it became established on its present site. I very much hope you will be able to join in as much of this as you can! Not every year can boast such an array of prime events as the time when the advent of this particular mark of remembrance can be turned to the glory of the fine name of St. Cretien's.

As we discussed last week, your teaching responsibilities would involve your taking on a number of classes right through the age-groups, and may include an Upper Sixth French class, as well as a little Russian and German. I am sure that Reginald Pompomery will contact you soon, in order to confirm the details exactly. As we also agreed at the interview stage, we would be very happy to try to accommodate you within the school, probably in a resident tutor's flat in one of our Boarding Houses. So far, it looks likely that you may be assigned to Welting House.

Thank-you once again for coming along to St. Cretien's for your interview, and I trust to see you again soon. Congratulations, too, for having been so successful in your application. And might I also take this opportunity to remind you again to ignore the recent coverage of the school in the press; there is absolutely no foundation at all for those particular allegations.

Yours sincerely,

A. K. Warble

ALAN WARBLE, BA CANTAB, Dip Ed

19 Semmingbury Way,
Canonsborough,
Herefordshire

23rd February, 2009

The Head Master,
St. Cretien's School,
West Sussex

Dear Mr. Warble,

Thank-you very much indeed for your kind letter of the 20th, and may I take this opportunity to say how much I appreciated my day out at St. Cretien's; I thoroughly enjoyed myself. Of course, I would be delighted to accept the offer and I look forward to coming to work at the school, despite the pupils.

Needless to say, I am certainly immensely excited by the prospect of starting my new job, and indeed life, at St. Cretien's, not least as I do not know the area thereabouts particularly well. In view of this, I intend to visit the school in a few months' time, in order to get to see the place in a more relaxed frame of mind!

I chatted with Mr. Pompomery about this, as the Head of French, and he suggests I come down sometime in May. I shall be staying with him in Dreer House for a couple of days, and will probably use my time to explore the various areas of school life, and to observe a few lessons. What I have seen so far of St. Cretien's seems to be most promising, and I look forward to getting to know more about the place in the near future! I feel that the school has a great deal of character, especially given its forthcoming celebrations, which I am sure will be a superb event for everyone.

I have also given some thought as to what clubs/activities I could become involved with. I was hoping that I might be able to help set up some sort of a Young Entrepreneurs Club, with a view to introducing the pupils to the basic ideas of business and money management; this does, I feel, tie in very closely with my interest in long-term weather patterns, and it could fit in well with applying such patterns to practical decisions, as we discussed at some length in our conversation over lunch. I hope this idea appeals to you.

Thank-you once more, and I hope to see you when I next come to St. Cretien's.

Yours sincerely,

Henry Pukeman

Flat No. 2, Dreer House,
St. Cretien's College,
West Sussex

FROM THE
HEAD OF MODERN LANGUAGES

23rd February, 2009

Dear Henry,

My sincerest congratulations on your appointment as *magister linguarum* here at St. Cretien's! My colleagues and I feel you will fit in admirably.

On the teaching front itself, you will be taking mainly French sets, as we discussed, as well as a little Russian. I believe that Mr. Gary Fraughter, Head of German, might like you to take a couple of German sets too, though, typically, he has not as yet communicated this specifically to me, and I am waiting for him to confirm this. Of course, your duties, it ought to be remembered, lie primarily and above all with the French Department; put simply, it is I who am your, as it were, *Line Manager*.

No doubt you will have a not inconsiderable wealth of questions and queries, and I trust you will communicate these to me and to my colleagues when you come to visit again. In fact, I would certainly recommend, on reflection, a few days' stay *in loco* at the school, in order to become familiar with things *in situ*, as it were. Perhaps you might be so kind as to drop me a line *à propos* of this later in the Spring, so that we can arrange your coming here *in medias res*. It may also be useful for you to see the type of accommodation available in the School; the Head Master told me yesterday that he was thinking of accommodating you in the Resident Tutor's flat in Welting House, which is something you will no doubt wish to consider. Do think about it, though it's not something you need to tell us *hic et nunc*.

On the whole, though, despite the odd query and concern you may have, I would recommend you not to worry overduly about how things will pan out here, once you arrive at St. Cretien's. I am sure that simply rolling up your sleeves and getting stuck in will be the best way to work out how the place ticks – that's how most of us here found our feet, and pretty well all the staff here are even less qualified than you are!

So, in the meantime, enjoy the improving weather (but don't read too much into it!) and let me know when you would be able to come again to St. Cretien's!

Yours sincerely,

R H Pompomery

R. H. POMPOMERY

ST. CRETIEN'S COLLEGE
WEST SUSSEX

FROM THE SECOND MASTER

Second Master's Lodge,
26th May, 2009

Dear Henry,

I was so very glad indeed to meet you again just recently, during your few days' visit to St. Cretien's, and I do very much hope you found the place to your liking the second time round! I am sure you will be very happy here, I know a number of long-term staff here who claim to be.

I include what I hope is very exciting information concerning your first year here. Along with all the rather boring stuff which you will need to fill in for our records (we need a CRB check, an enhanced CRB check, an extended CRB check, a region-specific alert-flag, a prison disclaimer, a ten-year address-confirmation check, an itemised expenses list from any previous employers, an intensive priority slide, a pro-biotic sample grade, a dry-needle DNA insertion, a unitary i-gloss, a local authority site-wide public disorder disclaimer, a substances and toxins statutory reading, a full firewall disclosure certificate, a pre-inception mandate from the passport office, a piece of inimate clothing with your scent on it, four utilities bills and, finally, your shoe size (one can never be too careful, these days!)), I also enclose a number of documents regarding the forthcoming events celebrating our sesquicentennial (150th!) anniversary here at St. Cretien's, as well as the new Prospectus, specially printed for the festivities! I do hope you'll take some time to look over these, not least as we shall be hoping you can fully involve yourself in all these unforgettable events. It really is promising to be a very fine beginning to the school year, as we celebrate the founding of the school in 1859.

St. Cretien's has a very long and proud history, and I am sure we are about to witness an exceptional term of remarkable, historic celebrations. For instance, each Boarding House is intending to put on some sort of event for the rest of the school, based on the number 150, or connected in some way with the date of our anniversary. Full details, of course, will be released at the staff meeting on Monday 7th September, where we will be able to welcome you formally to the Staff Common Room.

This will also be a time for you to be made aware of the various measures being followed up as the school prepares for quite a serious Toffsted Inspection, especially given the eventual outcome last time we had a go at one of these.

Furthermore, I have been led to believe that you are hoping to set up a Young Entrepreneurs Club, too, which I know the Head Master thinks will be a simply wonderful undertaking for those pupils at St. Cretien's with a business head on them! Do please keep us informed about this! I know it is something that the school will take very seriously, and I am sure the pupils will respond wonderfully to the idea.

In the meantime, do enjoy your summer, and I look forward to seeing you again once the new school year begins! Do enjoy looking at the Prospectus.

Yours sincerely,

Peregrine I. Grueson

DATES AND TIMES FOR THE START OF MICHAELMAS TERM 2009

Monday, September 7th

9.30am	Staff Meeting in Common Room, concerning the 150th Celebrations
11.00am	Common Room Meeting in the Common Room.
11.30am	Coffee Break.
12.00 noon	Short talk by guest speaker Dr. Trevelyan Whipsnash, Head Master of King William School, Cambs.

Subject: *Making the most of a mess - how to cope with incompetent staff.*

1.00pm	Lunch in the Dining Hall.
2.00pm	INSET Training: *How to Mark Work*. Presentation by Mrs. Primula Crown, with particular emphasis on what kind of pens to use in order to get the pupils to read your comments, but without feeling threatened.
5.00pm	Pupils begin arriving back for the start of term.
6.00pm	Dinner.
8.00pm	Roll Call in Boarding Houses.
10.30pm	Lock-up time.

Tuesday, 8th September

8.30am	Chapel for whole School.
9.30am	Lessons begin as per normal day.

PIG: 30/08/09

St. Cretien's College

OFFICIAL PROSPECTUS

An Independent School for Boys and Girls

Bringing a timeless education to 21st Century Children

SESQUICENTENNIAL EDITION

St. Cretien's College

St. Cretien's College, founded exactly one-hundred-and-fifty years ago in 1859 is set in the green and rolling hills of Sussex. It is a fully co-educational, independent boarding school, offering a rounded education to a pupil body of about 550 pupils. The staff at St. Cretien's pride themselves on maintaining a comfortable and friendly atmosphere in which your children can develop academically to the very best of their abilities, regardless of how disappointing that may eventually seem. Our pupils come from a variety of different backgrounds and cultures, without prejudice. We also welcome pupils of all faiths and denominations, and have a statutorily compliant policy on disability discrimination. Please feel free to contact the Headmaster's Secretary if you would like to visit St. Cretien's College, or visit our website at **www.stcretiens.org.uk** and follow our upcoming sesquicentennial celebrations on Twitter! - @stcretiens

This year St. Cretien's College is not only celebrating our **Sesquicentennial Jubilee**, which in itself is going to be a magnificent series of unforgettable events, but later in the school year, in April, the school is also having a full **Toffsted Inspection**. All of which means it's going to be quite a full year indeed!

Some Notable Old Cretians

There are too many Old Cretians, who have gone on to become lasting figures in the Pantheon of the Great and the Good, but here are some of the most illustrious and infamous of our alumni!

Benjamin Austen, *1935 - 1985*	Explorer of the foothills behind the East Russian city of Yakutsk. Opened up new yak-skin trading routes between Yakutsk, Okhotsk and Vladivostok. Ambushed and killed by local ferret mafia.
Fiona Bibble, *1956 –*	Leader of the arch-feminist *Worthing Independence Party* from 1978-80, after which she moved to the USA to join the presidential campaigns trail for Ronald Reagan.
Joseph "Sunny" Boyce, *1890– 1957*	Little-known inventor of the first atomic bomb in 1939, a primitive, enriched-uranium device, for which he tried in vain to obtain government backing
Owen Crack, *1936– 1998*	North Norfolk bog-snorkelling champion for seven years running, 1956-62
Penelope Dawes, *1977 -*	Well-known local figure jailed in 1992 for the triple murder of her business associates. Earned the soubriquet *The Spitting Vixen* for her methods of putting the police off her trail.
Otto von Gaukel, *1902 – 1968*	Educated between the wars at St. Cretien's, this divisive figure became *Generalfeldmarshall* of the German High Command, the *Wehrmachtführungsstab*, during WWII: despite being on the wrong side, he counts as one of St. Cretien's most successful alumni! Died in prison in East Berlin
Sir Edmund Gower, *1853 – 1921*	Founding member of the notorious *Semolina Club*, which rose to prominence in 1903 for publicly advocating a pre-emptive attack on Russia.
Margaret Hopes, *1935 -*	Academic and leading Oxford Theologian, whose major works include the seminal *Problems of Divine Intervention within a Modern Context of Post Soviet Socialist Realities.*
Orlando Hummus, *1845– 1924*	Orientalist and specialist in Middle Eastern affairs, creator of the popular dip made from mashed chickpeas, olive oil and tahini, which he named *orlandus*, after himself
Neville Hunker, *1879– 1945*	Legendary spy during both world wars, who managed to secure details in 1918 of German revolts (during which he lost his right leg), and who was in Japan at the end of the war, helping the Americans to pinpoint their bombing targets

Samuel Kriel, *1844 – 1907*   Assistant Vice-Deputy Secretary to the Home Secretary, Henry Bruce, 1872-73.

Salmo Lyttle, *1908– 1981*   Ballet impresario with the South Sidcup Amateur Dramatic Association of Dance; internationally renowned for his infamous *hoof-step*

Saviour Mandlebatt, *1936 – 1984*   Inventor of the modern harness strap for automatic cow-milking machines. Nominated for the Queen's Agricultural Award for Development and Innovation.

Selwyn Massmann, *1944 – 2004*   Mountain climber of international repute. Most recently (July, 2004) climbed Ben Nevis dressed as a dalek, to raise money for charity. Sadly, this was to be his last climb, as he died of heat-exhaustion on the way down.

Dwenge M'Boatang, *1932 -*   Activist and eventual first President of the newly independent, but short-lived African republic of Ngongo-Banandaland in 1964. In exile since 1970, believed to be living in Kashmir.

Yvonne O'Blong, *1950 –*   Campaigner for improved rights for trees, and instrumental in preventing the destruction of Wendown Woods in 1987

Bulimer Pancras, *1898– 1973*   Under-assistant General Secretary to the Second Chief of Auxiliary Staff during the Phoney War

Sir Brice Tylor, *1878 – 1940*   Inventor of the much-maligned *Bending Bomb* in WWII. Earlier awarded the Order of the Knotted Cross (Third Class) by the then Abyssinian government.

Sammy "Thwack", *1974 -*   Currently presenting the children's TV programme *Splash 'n' Dip!* Head of Children's Entertainment at Saltdean Lido.

Filippo Tombola, *1892 – 1968*   Author and poet. Published a number of light children's classics, such as *The Egg Doctor* and *When Tigglebacks Went To The Fairy-Cake Market*. Later successes include the epic poem, *The Bleakness of Death's Dark Oblivion* and *Life's Cruel Betrayal*.

Earnest Wilkes, *1923 – 1990*   Composer. Works include light operas and the theme tune to the TV hit *Who's Ya Baby?*

Sidney Yowkes, *1967 –*   Aid worker in Eastern Denmark

School Life at St. Cretien's College

A typical day's routine at St. Cretien's College is exciting, exhilarating and not a little tiring. There is much to be said for children leading active, stimulating lives, and this is one thing they are sure to get at St. Cretien's. As we say here, *Busy Children Can Move Mountains!*

5.00	-	Mattins
5.15	-	Carillon
6.00	-	Morning Chapel in Lower Crypt
		Watermeadows Run, plus Steeplechase
7.00 – 8.15	-	Breakfast in Dining Hall
8.30 – 11.10	-	Lessons, Periods 1 - 7
11.10 – 11.30	-	Break
11.30 – 1.30	-	Lessons, Periods 8 - 14
1.35 – 2.30	-	Lunch in Dining Hall
2.45 – 4.45	-	Afternoon lessons, Periods 15 - 22
4.45 – 6.30	-	Afternoon activities
6.30 – 7.00	-	Dinner in Dining Hall
7.00	-	Roll Call in Boarding Houses
7.15 – 9.30	-	Prep Time
8.45	-	Bedtime for 3rd Form
9.00	-	Bedtime for 4th Form
10.00	-	Bedtime for 5th Form
10.15 – 10.45	-	Sixth Form Bar open for light refreshments
10.45	-	Bedtime for 6th Form
11.00	-	Lights out
10.45 – 2.30	-	Staff nightly patrols

St. Cretien's College Farm

St. Cretien's College has had a fully functioning school farm since it was set up by a former Latin master, Dennis Pucker, in 1983, and it has since become an integral part of school life, providing a plentiful supply of fresh eggs, milk, and a variety of crops and meat. Furthermore, the farm plays an important role for those pupils who work on it, enabling them to develop skills and a sense of responsibility which will go on to serve them well in aspects of later life, especially dealing with bullies.

The farm itself boasts three wonderful friesian cows, named Alexis, Krystle and Fallon, none of whom are in very good health at the moment, despite the attentions of our young bull, Blake. We also have fifteen chickens, who are regularly serviced by our cock, Marco Pollo, and there are also our two resident sows, Britney and Kylie. Recently, St. Cretien's acquired Albert, a rescue llama, abandoned by a local entrepreneur, and an ostrich, who has proven to be so hostile to everything and everyone around him/her, that we have been obliged to keep it enclosed for its own good in a small cage at the edge of the farm.

St. Cretien's College Full-Time Staff

Senior Management Team   Initials

Head Master	Dr. Alan Warble, BA CANTAB, Dip Ed	AKW
Second Master	Mr. Peregrine Grueson, BA Lancs	PIG
Director of Studies	Dr. Anthony Ingham, BA OXON	ASI
Bursar	Rtrd. Admr. Quentin Smythers	QXS
Senior Chaplain	Revd. Dr. Derek Caustick	DIC
Snr. House Master	Mr. David Farrow	DUF

St. Cretien's College Boarding Houses

No.	Name	Sex	Housemaster	Initials
1	Welting	Boys	Mr. Barry Kuller	BOK
2	Crawling	Girls	Miss. Rhiannon Ninn	RUN
3	Plucker's	Girls	Mrs. Marjorie Gagg	MUG
4	Hythe	Boys	Mr. Daffyd Fang	DAF
5	Dreer	Boys	Dr. David Farrow	DUF
6	Deeping	Boys	Mr. Andrew Garrett	AFG
7	Smeltdown	Boys	Mr. Timothy Munt	TMM
8	Glibb	Boys	Dr. Felix Rompant	FVR
9	Grilling	Girls	Mrs. Deidre Dragoon	DUD
10	Scanker's	Boys	Mr. Eamon Fuller	EFF
11	Cocker's	Plenty	Mrs. Fiona Derry	FAD

Assistant Masters (* = Head of Department)

English:			Room:	
	Dr. Geoffrey Gripe*	GGG		New 3
	Mr. Richard Pounde	RUMP		New 7
	Dr. Roger Pampo	RIP		New 6
	Mrs. Sylvia Welks	SOW		New 8
	Miss. Olga Formost	OFF		New 4
	Mr. Paul Powte	POP		New 9

History:	Dr. Titus Tongle*	TIT	W 5
	Dr. Ibrahim Farook	IVF	W 3
	Mr. Timothy Rent	TTR	W 1
	Mr. Thomas Horngold	TRH	W 4
	Mrs. Deborah Jacks	DDJ	W 2
Classics:	Mr. Geoffrey Bernay*	GOB	W 10
	Dr. Anthony Ingham	ASI	W 9
	Dr. Frederick Pine	FOP	W 6
	Dr. Jayne Peece	JAP	W 7
	Mr. Selwyn Tidy	SOT	W 8
Divinity:	Dr. Roger Tailor*	ROT	QQ 4
	Revd. Dr. Derek Caustick	DIC	QQ 1
	Revd. Frédéric Mercure	FEM	QQ 3
	Mrs. Christina Hell	CIH	QQ 2
French:	Mr. Reginald Pompomery*	RHP	QQ 12
	Dr. Arthur Georges	ASG	QQ 11
	Mr. Andrew Garrett	AFG	QQ 15
	Mrs. Samantha Rectoil	SER	QQ 14
	Mr. Henry Pukeman	HIP	QQ 13
	M. Jean-Jacques Gerbier	J-JG	-
German:	Mr. Gary Fraughter*	GAF	QQ 6
	Mrs. Yasmin Krähler	YUK	QQ 7
	Mr. Peter Dome	PID	QQ 8
	Frl. Inge Schloggenfeuerhauer,	IS	-
Geography:	Mr. Vernon Bottockson*	VOB	G 3
	Mrs. Patricia Monce	PWB	G 2
	Mr. Barry Kuller	BOK	G 5
	Mr. Simon D'Essise	STD	G 4
	Mr. Edward Slicone	EJS	G 1
Mathematics:	Dr. Frank Thorney*	FAT	E 2
	Dr. Jeremy Horror	JEH	E 5
	Mr. Eamon Fuller	EFF	E 6
	Miss. Petra Muckhall	PUM	E 4
	Mr. David Farrow	DUF	E 3
	Dr. Gwendoline Sorely	GAS	E 1
Physics:	Dr. Iain Browne*	INB	Sc 5
	Dr. Felix Rompant	FVR	Sc 7
	Dr. Natalie Pusey	NIP	Sc 6
	Mr. Timothy Munt	TMM	Sc 9
	Mr. Oscar Lowe	OWL	Sc 8

Chemistry:	Dr. Michael Storr*	MAS	Sc 2
	Mr. Rodney Power	RAP	Sc 1
	Dr. Peregrine Grueson	PIG	Sc 5
	Mrs. Fiona Derry	FAD	Sc 3
	Mr. Terence Samuels	TPS	Sc 4
Biology:	Mr. Salvador Faranco*	SMF	Sc 11
	Dr. Olivia Power	ONP	Sc 12
	Frl. Sonja Mangle	SNM	Sc 13
	Mr. David Swelling	DMS	Sc 14
ICT:	Mr. Hugh Gregory*	HUG	ICT
	Mr. Tony Adonals	TGA	ICT
	Mr. Raoul Heffer	RAH	ICT
Economics:	Mr. Ted Prentice*	TIP	New 2
	Mr. Daffyd Fang	DAF	Sc 10
	Miss. Sally Irrell	SUI	New 1
Music:	Mr. Trevor King*	THK	M 1
	Mr. Howard Orwell	HOO	M 2
	Mrs. Marjorie Gagg	MUG	M 3
	Ms. Janet Szconoaiakovsky	JISZ	M 4
Art:	Ms. Petra Fayed*	PUF	A 1
	Miss. Rhiannon Ninn	RUN	A 2
	Mrs. Emily Raw	EBR	A 4
	Ms. Sandra Grate	SAG	A 3
Drama:	Mr. Selwyn Almari*	SRA	Theatre
	Mrs. Katherine Howle	KH	Theatre
Archaeology:	Mr. Quentin Galante	QBG	A4
Sport & Games:	Mr. Ronald Savage	RBS	
Librarian:	Mrs. Gail Haggers	GBH	

We hope you have a wonderful visit to St. Cretien's College !

UF45567:wrm3

17/07/09

33\ref.16
Personal

ST. CRETIEN'S COLLEGE
WORKS AND MAINTENANCE DEPT.

Re: Staff Accommodation within St. Cretien's site

Dear Mr. Pukeman,

On behalf of the Health and Safety Working Committee (HSWC) here at St. Cretien's College, I should like to welcome you to your new position, and hope you are looking forward to working and living here. We hope we can provide you with everything you will need once you are here, but I am writing now to inform you of a number of details concerning everyday life here in such a community.

The Health and Safety Executive consists of myself, Brian Blouse, Head of Facilities Management and Barry Soddum, the Head Manager of Facilities.

Together, we manage a rolling programme of Health and Safety priority assessment and strategic implementation within a global community structure of management implementation and structural management under the umbrella structure of the St. Cretien's Health and Safety Works Committee (HSWC).

In a place like St. Cretien's, where the safety of the pupils and staff is paramount, there is a great deal of emphasis placed on Health and Safety, and the HSWC is frankly dogged in its implementation of these necessary regulations, which serve to make St. Cretien's a pleasant and safe environment in which to work. It should be added that in the school year 2008-2009, there was a total of only 14 serious injuries on the school site, only five of which resulted in permanent scarring or disabilities, and a mere 45 lesser incidents, most of which were down to incorrect assumptions in the individual's own risk assessments. We pride ourselves on this record, and see it as a direct result of the "best practice" pursued by Barry and myself.

We are aware that you will be moving into the Tutor's Flat in Welting House. This is an older property, and we would ask you to think very carefully about how much of a burden you are liable to put on such a structure and infrastructure. We would urge you, for instance, to use no more than one electrical appliance at any given time, including the heating. Please do not flush the toilet more than once a day, as this has been known to cause the dormitory below to flood with raw sewage on more than one occasion, which could leave the school open to litigation.

On an even more serious note, could you please refrain from having more than two guests in the flat at any one time, as the beams in Welting House are known to be over a hundred years old now, and there is a definite risk of collapse due to an often overlooked condition in untreated wood of that age, namely *retchworm*. In any case, it would also be advisable not to entertain any two guests whose combined weight were to exceed 36st on any upstairs floors in the school, as our current insurance as regards *retchworm* has recently expired. With this in mind, please could you pass on your own vital statistics to us here at the Health and Safety Office, so that we can ascertain the various potential risks your own body weight might pose to the pupils and staff working below you.

Both Barry and myself are always available for discussion regarding any aspect of the working environment here at St. Cretien's. Our office is located behind the temporary toilets next to the Half Pipe (soon to be removed for Health and Safety reasons).

Brian Blouse, GWTO, c/o HSWC

BB : 17/07/09

FROM
ST. CRETIEN'S COLLEGE
SECURITY

PLEASE NOTE

**By agreeing to move into a Tutor's Flat
you have automatically consented to the Security
Doctrine, as drawn up under the terms of the St. Cretien's
Security Committee 2003. Under these terms your movements
within the school might at any time be monitored by CCTV,
and any relevant footage which could implicate you in
criminal activity will be passed on to the police
and pursued through the legal system.**

**The camera at the entrance to your flat should not pose any
threat to you leading a normal life, as long as you do not
engage in any illegal activities, and it should be noted that
details of any guests and visitors will also be recorded**

**The parking space for your vehicle has now been registered as
Lot No. 13, at the far end of the Lower Rugby Fields.**

Thank-you and enjoy your life here

in St. Cretien's!

The St. Cretien's

Christian
Union

WELCOMES A NEW SOUL

Yo, BRO' !!

Greetings to YOU in your new HOME !!

Come and join us every week for prayers, *talks* and some serious huggin' love for our _Lord_

JESUS CHRIST

**Every Thursday in the Crypt
@ 7.30**

Enrol now for the <u>Arouse!</u> _Course_, and <u>bring</u> buddies

**We all need savin' and when better to start?
New job, new home, NEW LIFE !!!**

It gonna be just like bein'

BORN AGAIN

HALLELULIA !!!

```
X-ViruChekked: Checked
From: Hip@stcretiens.org.uk
Date: Mon, 24 Aug 2009 15:38:05 EST
Subject: New School
To: royandbrenda@yahoo.co.uk
X-Mailer: CompuServ 2001 6.0 for Windeyes UK sub 233309
X-MD-d: royandbrenda@yahoo.co.uk X-Return-Path:
hip@school@stcretiens.org.uk
Reply-To: hip@school@stcretiens.org.uk
```

royandbrenda@yahoo.co.uk

Dear Mum and Dad,

Oh my God, what a load of quirky characters! I was expecting there to be a few odd-bods, like anywhere, I'm sure; I suspect this kind of institution encourages a bit of eccentricity. So far so good... But some of my colleagues do look like they've stepped straight out of another era altogether!

The place clearly wants to put on a good show, mind you. I can't believe how beautiful it is! I know you saw it a bit when you dropped me off last week, but the countryside just round-about is gorgeous, and you can see why staff would end up spending their whole lives teaching here! They also have marvellously long holidays (this past summer break was 14 weeks long!) so they all head off, sometimes on school trips with the pupils, to the most exotic and dangerous places. Last night I met a colleague who has just come back from touring Antarctica and Patagonia with a small group of Fourth Formers! Ostensibly a geography field trip...

What's more, everyone's also been talking up the whole 150th celebration thingy, so that's going to be quite a show for the first few months here! At least it might take away some of the bad publicity from the leaky gas problems they've been having, and that attack with the iron bar. Sounds like they were just quite isolated incidents, to be honest. Anyway, they've got a school inspection looming now, so that'll be fun!

Hope you have a good holiday next week, I'll be thinking of you both.

Let me know how things go, and I'll get in touch when you get back. I'll probably be up to visit at half term. Or you come down to me, I've got the spare room, it wouldn't be any hassle.

Well, I've only got a week or so now until the first pupils arrive. A few are coming early for sports training, as well as the prefects who are quite active setting stuff up at the beginning of the year. And then in a week or so's time, we'll see what it's like standing in front of a proper class for the first time! Should be fun! Can't wait, after all that training I've done, and actually to have my own class! Bound to be a bit weird at first, but kind of exciting to be in control of real classes doing real things!

Also, I've been told I can set up a Young Enterprise-style lunchtime club, so that should be fun!

with much love,

Henry

MICHAELMAS TERM

September, 2009

Jul. 2009
Hello Head Master, Just a quick greeting
to let you know what is going on in the
German Dept, in case you had forgotten
you had one, and to reassure you that
no pupil has been lost this time, nor
burned, nor attacked by pockets of
WWII resistance still hiding out in
the woods, nor swept out to sea (we're
staying in Bavaria, in case you'd
forgotten), nor abducted by aliens, nor
come to any harm at all. Hope you're enjoying
your relaxing holidays. See you next term,   Gary

The Head Master
The Master's Lodge
Sedgwickham,
West Sussex,

July 2009   Dear Head Master, Hello from myself,
Simon D'Essise and the seven boys we
have brought to Paris on our rather
indulgent art trip to the Louvre. It has been
worthwhile so far, wtih the pupils really
engaging with the works we're looking at,
and enjoying the chance to immerse them-
-selves completely in it all – we've so
far managed to stay in after closing hours
three times now, and had the run of the
place after dark, which puts a totally new
perspective on it all! Planning another lock-in
tonight, got our hiding-place all sorted!

The Head Master
The Master's Lodge
Sedgwickham,
West Sussex,
Angleterre

Anthony

July '09

Dear Head Master, A merry message of salutations from many merry children and myself just to let you know that all is going very well indeed on our Classics Grand Tour so far! The three minibuses are holding up, though one of them did overheat a bit, on the outskirts of Sparta. Never mind, all in a day's work (even in our holidays!) Hope you're enjoying yours!

Antony & Jayne

The Head Master
The Master's Lodge
Sedgwickham,
West Sussex,
Αννλιά

July '09

Dear Head Master, A quick Hello from Howard, Marjorie, Gail, Peter, Bob and myself, as well as from the three pupils we've brought here to Salzburg for the 253rd Mozart celebrations. We've made it to seven excellent concerts so far, and I've already got some ideas for this year's concerts. The boys have bought you some Mozart Balls.

Yours, Trevor

The Head Master
The Master's Lodge
Sedgwickham,
West Sussex,
Grossbritannien

July '09

Dear Headmaster

Hope you're enjoying your summer holidays. We certainly are having a lovely time here doing our tour of the Central European Concentration camps. Tomorrow we will be doing Dachau, then off to see the second part of the Ring Cycle. Should be fun.! At the weekend will visit site of Nuremberg rallies, then back home in time for the Christian Union trip to Taíz It never stops! Barry Kuller

The Head Master
The Master's Lodge
Sedgwickham,
West Sussex,
England

Aug, 09

Warmest greetings from the filthiest protest camp I've ever taken a school group to! It's massive here, though, with 100's of young people causing mayhem for the US authorities! Hope we've been seen on TV by now! The air here is positively revolutionary! Your daughter's fine, by the way, and loving every minute! Must go now, as we've been asked to converge on MacDonald's at noon... Didn't do a risk-assessment for this, oops!! See you next term, Daffyd Fang

The Head Master
The Master's
Lodge
Sedgwickham,
West Sussex,
UK

Aug, 09   Forest Camp,
                               Bucks
Sir, All Present and Correct and
nothing amiss to report. The St
Cretien's CCF has been on excellent
form this week, and all my fellow
officers in the mess have congratulated
me and the school in producing such
excellent young killing machines. I
hope you are as delighted as I am.
Jackson in particular has shown
himself to be very ruthless indeed on the
night patrols. See you in September.
                        Tony Adonals

The Head Master
The Master's
Lodge
Sedgwickham,
West Sussex,

Aug 09
Dear Head Master
Everything here is fine, and
Mr. Rent says we should be
back pretty soon, maybe by
Half Term! We are being treated
very decently by our captors,
and nobody has been hurt yet.
Please don't worry at all.
Columbia's really lovely.
                    Shelly Fudge

The Head Master
The Master's Lodge
Sedgwickham,
West Sussex,
Inglaterra

<u>AGENDA FOR STAFF MEETING</u>

Monday, 7th September, 2009

1. Welcoming of new staff

2. Head Master's business, as follows:

    - News of last year's GCSE and A-Level results
    - Talk on improvement of standards and work ethos amongst staff
    - Unveiling of planned extension to Head Master's Lodge, to include space for conferences and retail zone
    - Cut-backs; staff biscuits in Common Room to consist of plain assortment only; change of coffee to Waitrose's own brand
    - Latest news on Timothy Rent, still lost on Fourth Form Expedition to the Amazon; last reported sighting of him and his group was in Colombia with troop of jungle guerrillas
    - Looming Inspection – no need to say any more

3. Bursar's business, as follows:

    - Balance of payments. General situation
    - Recent difficulties: Last year's 500-page Magazine, plus glossy photo-supplement to celebrate the College's Sesquicentennial Anniversary.
    - Expenses involved in the Summer Term's Staff Trip to Calais, including the parking fines and bail
    - Further discussion of Common Room extravagances and expenses, especially regarding biscuits, coffee and newspapers - urgent need to redress balance
    - Decision to use the Great Hall for a special Christmas event laid on by organisers *Swing Now!*

4. Second Master's business:

    - Unveiling of the final plans for the entire Sesquicentennial Anniversary Celebrations – memo put up on Notice Board, please read in full
    - Implementation of "Crisis Management Plan 617" (see Staff Handbook, pg. 63, para. 3) in preparation for the impending Inspection. This will need a serious thinking-through of all the measures we have put in place for it during the last three terms.
    - Increase in pupils smoking – memo put up on Notice Board, please read in full
    - Staff smoking patrols - the need to extend them into the holidays
    - Behaviour in Dining Hall - especially staff
    - Fire practices - the next is to take place on Sunday at 3.30am; all resident staff are expected to be present and to help

5. Chaplain's business
6. Senior Master's business
7. Director of Studies

30/08/09:PIG

Mr. Grueson at work in his lab

ST. CRETIEN'S COLLEGE
WEST SUSSEX

FROM THE SECOND MASTER

RE: 150th ANNIVERSARY

RE: 150th ANNIVERSARY

Second Master's Lodge,
28th August, 2009

To all staff:

It has been decided through the Senior Management Team (SMT), the Events Committee, the PTA and the Committee for the Sesquicentennial Jubilee that the commemorations should begin on Sunday 20th September, which actually marks the date that Lord Buncombe of Blithery laid the Foundation Stone of St. Cretien's College. So that Sunday will be set aside as Extraordinary Founder's Day, with parents invited to come to a special morning Chapel Service, followed by the prize-giving ceremony that had to be postponed last term because of the gas leak. Then we will finish with a picnic lunch on the Main Quad, or in the Cloisters if the weather is inclement.

During the afternoon, we shall witness a number of the events organised by each individual Boarding House, around the idea of "150 years." Obviously not all of them can be done there and then. Below is a list of what each House is planning to do:

1   Welting   -   The entire House is doing a sponsored swim of 150 lengths all together in the swimming pool – renamed "The Sesquicentennipool" for the day

2   Crawling   -   The pupils are building a number of full-size papier-maché hot-air balloons, which they will charge pupils and parents for a ride in on Sunday afternoon, though not out towards the sea

3   Plucker's   -   Whole House to sing a great choral anthem at one-minute to seven (18:59 – well done if you spotted it, I didn't!). In order to make it accessible, it will be to the theme tune of *Titanic*, and to give it added gravitas, the text will be in Latin, from a Latin version of *Asterix and the Big Fight* – whole school to attend

4   Hythe   -   150 fireworks to be let off from the roof of Hythe House

5   Dreer   -   Before the Sunday festivities, the pupils of this House are going to decorate all the trees on the site by wrapping and painting their trunks in the school colours

6   Deeping   -   The House has made a Time Capsule, which will be buried at a ceremony on Sunday afternoon, and not opened until 2159

7   Smeltdown   -   Will ring the House Bell located in the turret above the TV room 150 times slowly over three hours

8   Glibb   -   The House is promising to do all manner of good deeds over the following week for the elderly residents of Sedgwickham

9	Grilling	-	The House is presenting a mural to the Head Master, to be erected at the north end of the Meaddings Hall, to celebrate the history and the life of the school
10	Scanker's	-	One single member of the House, Alvin Gawker, has learned the entire Iliad, by Homer, in the original, and he is intending to recite it to the school, maybe not on that Sunday, but on another day we might be able to set aside; other members of his House have been suspiciously happy to take a back seat in all this, but Alvin's enthusiasm for Ancient Greek has cheerfully won the day. Quite what the Iliad has to do with St. Cretien's I don't know, but anyway, that is the contribution from Scanker's House...
11	Cocker's	-	To commemorate the 1859 solar eclipse, the entire House is attempting to recreate the event by wearing sunglasses

Over the course of the following two weeks, a number of other, discrete events will take place, including a school concert with music specially written for our new School Hymn, a special staff v. pupils quiz, the unveiling of a new School Prayer at Sunday Chapel on the 27th September (we had hoped to have it ready by the 20th, but Revd Caustick tells me he won't have written it by then, and he assures me he'll need a lot of time to meditate on the words in order to get it right).

The fortnight of celebrations will reach a climax on Saturday 3rd October, when the entire school will process from the Chapel out to Sedgwickham, in order to attend a short open-air ceremony, followed by the unveiling of a plaque on the wall of the *Hare and Hounds*, which was, of course, the place where our founder started teaching the children, who would later become the first actual pupils of St. Cretien's College.

Afterwards, the school will then process back, and the evening will be marked by a giant hog roast on the Back Quad, and the whole event crowned with Welting House's grand firework display, as mentioned above!

I don't know about you all, but I can hardly wait! This is going to be a very memorable few weeks in St. Cretien's history, which will amply make up for some of the recent disappointments we have had landing on our doorstep. Please do sign up for as many of the events as you can, in order to have as many hands as possible on deck!

Thank-you all in advance for your support in all this – together we can make this special.

Peregrine I. Grueson

28/08/09: PIG

COMMON ROOM MINUTES for September, 2009
Special Meeting with PIG regarding special sesquicentennial arrangements

Taken by R. M. Pounde

To begin with, the Common Room welcomed new members of staff, Mr. Selwyn Tidy (SOT), to teach Classics, Mr. David Swelling (DMS), joining the Biology Dept., Mrs. Christina Hell (CIH), for Religious Studies, Mr. Henry Pukeman (HIP), French and Russian, Ms. Janet Szconoaiakovsky (JISZ) and Mr. Raoul Heffer (RAH); also welcomed were Jean-Jacques Gerbier, the French *assistant* as well as Inge Schloggenfeuerhauer the German *Assistentin*.

The meeting proper then began with the Second Master (PIG) outlining a number of issues that had arisen as a result of various problems the previous term. These had all, he reminded us, ended up generating a certain amount of adverse publicity in the local press, and even made it into one or two national papers. As a result, the Head Master wants it to be known that he intends this year to be a "disaster-free year" and for there to be no major mishaps.

Perhaps the most notable event of the previous term had been the gas leak, and more importantly the failure of the school to notify the relevant authorities. Apparently, by the time it was finally detected hanging over most of nearby Sedgwickham, the emergency services were loath to believe that it had in fact originated from two-and-a-half miles away, and claimed they were astonished that no harm had actually been done. Well, in fact, a great deal of harm had been done, to the tune of just over £456,000 loss to the school's finances. Our local Police Liaison Officer, PC Evelyn Hall, said that when the gas leak was discovered spreading over the area, officials likened it to spotting the first signs of radioactivity coming over Europe from Chernobyl. Apparently, we have to count our lucky stars that nobody lit any flames or sparks on the morning when it was at its worst, as it could have kept our fire brigade busy for days.

Needless to say, we can't afford the same thing to happen again, not just in terms of money, but also with the risk to life and limb. It wouldn't have been so bad, had it escaped from a faulty pipe, but the fact that one of the junior kitchen ovens was left on over a leave-weekend suggests negligence on the school's part.

On a still quite serious note, PIG also mentioned the increased incidence of pupils brewing and distilling their own drinks in their rooms. The situation is not in any way compliant with HMC guidelines, and what's more was the cause of lots of bleary-eyed pupils towards the end of term, when the routines of the timetable fizzled out, and left them with a lot of free time on their hands. Not only is it bound to be detrimental to the pupils' health, but it was also making a lot of staff on Saturday night patrols think that there was no longer a drinking culture in the school, given that the pupils were no longer smuggling booze onto the site. The fact that the Third Form in Scanker's House had actually set up a whole corner of their dormitory for the distillation of poteen, was, feels PIG, a low point in the school's record on discipline.

Likewise, please can all staff continue to clamp down on pets in the boarding houses – still no sign yet of the tarantula which escaped last April, and which happens to be particularly poisonous.

We had a lot of complaints last term regarding the use of fancy dress among the pupils, hiring out costumes from the local shop in Sedgwickham, and using them to frighten the juniors. Although we enjoyed a number of creative theme-nights and discos, it must be said that it was unfair of some our senior pupils to spend such a lot of energy telling scary stories about UFOs and local hauntings, only to terrify the younger ones in their rooms after dark. Some detentions are still pending in relation to these misdemeanours. Unfortunately, Ellie Hopes, a certain up-and-coming young journalist on the Sedgwickham Herald, decided to run with this particular "scoop," after little Earnest Gumper was found running naked across the village green claiming he'd been taken away by aliens, as opposed to being given vodka by the seniors and driven out to the woods behind Underwood Lane.

It has been decided that David Swelling (DMS) will be standing down from his traditional role as Master-in-Charge of Cross Country. This is mainly due to his having done it for so long that, along with the Head Master and the rest of the SMT, he feels he is no longer able to bring the required verve and zest to the activity. It might also have something to do with the fact that he has spent the last twenty years not actually running along the route he sends the pupils out on, and had not noticed the appearance of a busy, dual-carriageway bypass, built only fourteen years ago, which happens to cut across the route at two points. From next week, Michael Storr has kindly agreed to take on the role, on the understanding that he changes the route, and runs it at least once himself, in order to check there are no potential health and safety issues (or newly-built airport runways, for that matter) that might get the school into trouble.

A new girl, Sally Delver, is joining the Fourth Form, from St. Homberg's School, Withyhampton. It is understood she has had a few problems there; she has been advised that St. Cretien's is just the sort of place that could provide her with the stability she needs.

Finally, PIG reminded everyone present as Second Master that the Common Room's help in smoking patrols would be very much appreciated, not least as the problem had become a real issue last term, with more and more pupils being caught in possession of tobacco. PIG asked if there would be anyone willing to help him on the first graveyard slot of the term this coming Saturday night from 2:30 to 5:30 am. TMM volunteered.

The Director of Studies pointed out a few errors in the term diary: No bring-and-buy sale on Oct. 17th but a car-boot sale would still be held on the following Saturday afternoon, in the Lower Field if fine, if not then in the Grand Hall and perhaps stretching into the Meaddings Hall if necessary; the Third Form Observation Week would now be during the seventh week of term, and not in the ninth as advertised; Holy Communion Awareness Sunday had been moved to the previous week, in order to make way for Ladies' Bingo in the Meadding's Hall; and the deadline for AS and A Level exam entries would have to be on the 14th, not the 17th, as shown in the diary, because of the run-up to Oxbridge entry (though this particular year's Upper Sixth unfortunately seemed rather thin on the Oxbridge front).

The newspaper auction was then held.

- Minutes witnessed and signed off: RUMP & PIG

ST. CRETIEN'S COLLEGE
WEST SUSSEX

FROM THE SECOND MASTER

RE: SMOKING PATROLS

Second Master's Lodge,
23rd August, 2009

As I am sure you will all be very well aware, there have been many instances over the past academic year of successfully surprising those pupils of ours who deliberately continue to participate in the sordid habit of smoking. Although all colleagues have helped to patrol the school site with no unpleasant incidents, there is, I feel, space to introduce a number of new practices, which I outline below:

1. When on patrol, please ensure that members of staff wander around in groups of at least two, so as to ensure that there is at all times a witness in case the accused pupil decides to lodge an official complaint or in case s/he becomes aggressive.

2. Refrain from going on patrol in groups of three or more, as this can appear intimidating to the pupils caught smoking, especially those younger ones barely in their teens. I would also ask all staff not to appear too menacing when approaching a group of smokers, even though they are often to be found in groups of twenty or more, and tend to keep their hoods up and wear sunglasses. I would also remind staff that a number of smokers have described to me how they felt humiliated when staff made rather sarcastic comments to their (admittedly disguised) faces about the dangers of smoking - after all, we are on patrol to help them face their addiction, not to lecture them!!!

3. When a group is caught, remind them loud and clear that they are on School property, and that they form an integral part of the community of St. Cretien's. Then take a selection of their cigarettes (I suggest one from every three to four pupils, varying your range fairly between boys and girls, and ensuring that a broad spectrum is acquired from all year-groups present, as well as not picking on a whole group of pupils standing close by one another, in case other unrelated substances are being enjoyed (!) by other members within the group, but across the way), and take a minute drag from each, entering your results in the smoking book kept in the Common Room; I will collate these figures on a weekly basis, so as to ascertain whether or not we have a drugs problem here at St. Cretien's. If you are not sure as to the smell and taste of certain substances, I have a stash of confiscated, illegal material in the top drawer of my desk which I am happy to allow you to see when I am in my office.

4. Remember to enter the names and boarding house of the offenders, and to mention the incident to the pupil's House Master, who will deal with it internally: some pupils may even face the sanction of early bedtime.

23/08/09: PIG

<u>COMMON ROOM NOTICE BOARD</u>

Would the teachers who have any of the following pupils on their set lists please forward work to them via myself:

Fiona CALIBRATE	Crawling
Vincent CHANG-LI	Deeping
Sam CROOK	Dreer
Quentin EYESAW	Deeping
Shelly FUDGE	Plucker
Puocha ACHOO-MBARABCHAO	Scanker's
Gerard MUNGLE	Hythe
Frank RACHETT	Scanker's
Simon RASH	Hythe
Paula SIMBIOTICA	Crawling
Terence WANG	Dreer
William WOLLY	Deeping

These Fourth Formers are those currently trapped in Colombia with Timothy Rent, apparently holed up in a deserted village east of Neiva. Timothy has been in contact with David Arkwright and assures him that they are being well treated but are all now becoming quite exasperated. Many of the pupils would like to have something to take their minds off their ordeal, and Timothy is concerned that they may be falling behind on their work. Their captors have agreed to allow work to be sent to them, so if colleagues would be so kind as to pass on to me any exercises and worksheets they could be getting on with, this would be much appreciated. Naturally, they have limited resources where they currently are, and the word is that they may soon be on the move again, due to the political turmoil right now, so please keep the work simple enough to be done with basic pencils.

Timothy sends us his best wishes, and hopes to see us all soon. He hopes to be back by Half Term, not least because he has a holiday booked to spend the break in Kabul!

Anthony Ingham

Anthony Ingham, Director of Studies

Head Master's Speech Notes– Start of Michaelmas 2009

-wait for silence... Ex day-o gloria jew ventiss ett sap-yentis... pause... From the Lord cometh the glory of youth and of learning. Please be seated.

wait for settling down...

Thank-you. Welcome back. Well I hope you've all enjoyed the long summer holidays, and I hope you have come back to St. Cretien's well rested, reinvigorated and wholly ready for the beginning of a new school year. We ended last year on a somewhat sour note, you may remember, and loath as I am to begin the new term on a downbeat, as it were- pause, look around – I feel that the beginning of a new year allows us to judge all the more objectively the events of the previous. However, we must remember to turn off any gas ovens we use, and we must also be kinder to those less able to defend themselves, especially when they do not happen to be holding iron bars and radiator pipes.

short silence - allow for some guilty coughs and shuffles

yes, this is indeed the time to look at what St. Cretien's is, and this is first and foremost– tremulous pause – a community. A community of 500 plus pupils living alongside each other at all times of the day, not to mention alongside teaching staff, matrons, sports coaches and cleaners. And it is apt, therefore, for me to mention all facets of community life here, is it not, because, even though a number of boys were severely punished for what they did to Mrs. Huang-King from the cleaning department, I still feel much sadness that members of St. Cretien's could stoop so low in the way they kept and tortured her for that long. Bastards, quite frankly, and I do not use my words lightly.

broad sweep and v steely stare – wait for shock to die down – smile benignly but firmly

Nor is it acceptable that we have had to rebuild the Cricket Pavilion on Lower Fields, since its attic was used thoughtlessly by smokers, who unbelievably did not even think of how flammable thatch can be. I honestly do wonder how mindless some actions can seem with hindsight.

So, let us spend a little more time – shout this v loud – thinking a bit more before we act. Remember, what little thought you spend on others is magnified by the thoughts thought upon you by those same others, by dint of thinking the very thoughts you might like others to spend on you.

Long pause... straighten up – finger point

Well, let us go off now with that thought in our minds. Enjoy the beginning of this new term, and let's be strong in the way we approach whatever we do!

allow for massive applause to die away

Loud-artay educat-see-onem in nomminy domminy
Praise learning in the name of the Lord.

Right side first please, in an orderly fashion. Follow the monitors, thank-you

HM

Dr. Alan Warble
Head Master
—In full flow
during a school
assembly

School office memorandum – Common room notice board

Special Head Master's Detentions

2 . 9 . 09

This is a one-off punishment list for miscreants whose behaviour at the end of last year occurred too late to deal with

Wynn Chester	single	Smoking
Mag Daylene	double	Smoking
Gordon Stone	single	Dressing up as Dracula to scare 3rd Form
Ytona Row	double	Smoking
Edward King	single	Smoking
Eleanor Holls	single	Smoking
Lance Singh	single	Smoking
Bee Dayles	double	Dressing up as Frankenstein
Rob Hathe	single	Smoking
Heriot Fetters	single	Dressing up as a baby-eating zombie
Sven Øks	single	Smoking
Wes Minster	single	Smoking
Chris O'Spittle	single	Wearing a Nixon mask, checking up on juniors
Abby Ingdon	double	Dressing up as a mummy just before bedtime
Brad Fields	single	Pretending to be an alien on the roof of Welting
Wes Tonbert	single	Dressing up as corpse and lying in a cupboard
Mall Verne	single	Impersonating the Head Master
Glenn Armand	double	Smoking whilst dressed as a martian
Horace Hill	double	Being dressed as an evil clown whilst smoking

All detentions will take place in **TMM's room** (Science 9) from 7.30 pm till 10.00

San Francisco,
California, USA

The Head Master,
St. Cretien's College,
Sedgwickham, Sussex

14th August, 2009

Dear Mr. Warble,

        Further to our earlier correspondence, I am still very interested in the prospect of sending my daughter, Bella, to your establishment but would like to know a little more about the entrance exam. I had understood that there is an expectation that my daughter would need to prove her IQ to be above 35, and I do worry that we will not have enough time to coach her to that level before interviews next month.

As you know, Bella currently boards at a local Academy but is beginning to become rather flabby in her whole approach to life, if you know what I mean. I do want her to be able to pursue her real passions, which are French and Drama, and I feel England would do her some good. She has shown herself to be occasionally wanton in her behaviour, and we both feel she needs to be brought out of herself.

The good news is I have had confirmed the possibility of a federal grant, and it seems that, given the type of work we do here, there will be some quite considerable funds available, enough to cover Bella's School fees. However, I would need from St. Cretien's confirmation that your school is in no way involved in anti-democratic subversive activities and that you have no intent to overthrow the presidency of the United States. If you can confirm this by replying to my wife's address, my guys can put it in the correct format. I am between addresses right now and I cannot reveal my location at present.

Bella is working hard to get herself up to scratch to come to an English school of your standing, and God willing, I think she will do it. She is so keen on becoming a Cretian, where she can learn more French and Drama - her particular favourites.

God Bless,

Kind regards

Havey O'Nyons

[48]

The Master's Lodge,
Sedgwickham,
West Sussex,

2nd September, 2009

Dear Mr. O'Nyons,

Thank-you for your last letter, and I am very sorry not to have got back to you before now, but, as you have probably surmised, we have not long been back from our fourteen-and-a-half weeks summer holidays.

Thank-you for your interest in St. Cretien's, but I am pleased to tell you that there was no cause for alarm, as the information I passed on to you was totally correct, and still stands as per my initial response. Fees begin at £17,500 per year, which is US$49,500 (per term).

In order for your daughter Bella to qualify for entry as a Cretian, she would indeed need to have an IQ of above 35, and be able to throw and catch medicine balls in a physical co-ordination and aptitude test. If you do have any relevant French or Drama work of Bella's which you would like to pass on to us electronically, please do so, it would be a pleasure to see it.

Considering your own profession, you might be interested to know that there are a number of children at St. Cretien's whose parents are likewise big names in the fruit and vegetable business, including the heir to the Riora fortune, and the three sons of Onions 4 The World, an influential organic vegetable conglomerate here in South-east England.

As regards the stuff about St. Cretien's not being anything but above-board, you have my word that nothing untoward goes on here.

All my very best, and looking forward to hearing from you in due course. I do hope that Bella will be able to join us here at St. Cretien's soon, as this promises to be a very memorable year indeed, with the school on the cusp of celebrating the Sesquicentennial (150th) Anniversary of its foundation!

PS: Early enrolment could lead to a 2.5% discount in fees.

Yours sincerely,

A. K. Warble

ALAN WARBLE, BA CANTAB, Dip Ed

THE ST. CRETIEN'S

DEBATING SOCIETY

FIRST DEBATE OF THE YEAR!!

Please join us in the Library for this first debate,
followed by tea, coffee and biscuits

This week's motion:

THIS HOUSE BELIEVES THAT EDUCATION FOR THE MASSES IS A COMPLETE AND UTTER WASTE OF TIME

*

Thursday, 7.30 pm

Please ensure you obtain your Housemaster's / Housemistress' permission
beforehand

The Master's Lodge,
Sedgwickham,
West Sussex,

10th September, 2009

<u>To all staff</u>

<u>Re: September 11th Anniversary</u>

The tragic events which occurred in 2001 are to be remembered in a special chapel service this Friday evening at 7.00, where the Revd Caustick will speak to the whole school, and at which prayers shall be said for world peace.

On the world stage, I like to think, a school such as ours still kicks above its weight, and it will strengthen our pupils to see that St. Cretien's is making a palpable difference. In so many ways, I feel that the school needs to be seen to be addressing these issues, providing our pupils with the chance to engage with the world outside our cloisters, as well as providing, as it were, spiritual value for money in a fee-paying milieu. What's more, we happen to have a small delegation of American guests visiting this week, who are keen to forge links with St. Cretien's, and who are we to stand in the way of the great market economy?

Many thanks in advance for your presence tomorrow evening.

A. K. Warble

ALAN WARBLE, BA CANTAB, Dip Ed

12th September

CRNB

In response to the sermon preached yesterday by the Chaplain, and as a pro-active member of a country still calling itself a democracy, I am setting up a Peace Cave in the Science Block lobby. All pupils and staff are welcome to drop in whenever they feel like it, where I hope they will find a contemplative space more suited to some than the coldness of a chapel built on the back of colonial crimes against humanity. The situation in New York was indeed tragic, as the HM says, but it is precisely against the hegemony of a pseudo-fascist, imperialist America that my Economics masterclass and I went to New York last month, and why we needed to smash at the very heart of their evil empire. I don't condone what happened there, but I do think the pupils here need to see the other side of the argument, and so do drop by if you like. We shall be organising some face-painting and baking cakes this evening to start off our protest.

All the best,

Daffyd Fang

Head Master, Second Master

St. Cretien's Combined Cadets Forces

Tony G. Adonals

Dear Sirs,

I am writing to test the waters with an idea that some of the pupils here in CCF have suggested to me, and that is a CCF trip this coming Easter to help our troops in Afghanistan. This could be part of a 150th Anniversary celebratory trip, to tie in with all the involvement St. Cretien's has had over the years with the military.

Obviously, there would be a number of things to consider beforehand, not least in terms of risk-assessment, but I do feel it would be a valuable experience for the boys and girls, it would show them a lot about real life in the armed forces, and it could be a small PR stroke of genius, as it would show St. Cretien's off in a very positive (even glamorous) light, upholding some of the values that our public schools used to be so proud of.

There is the small matter of transport, as I don't think any of our minibuses would be up to that kind of distance, and it would be a journey which passes through some pretty hazardous parts of the world. But once in Afghanistan, I do know of an excellent military training camp just outside Kabul, and a mate of mine in the Army says he would even be able to organise for some of our more adventurous pupils to join the boys in action, and at least a day-trip out to the Hindu Kush.

Hoping for a positive reply.

ST. CRETIEN'S COLLEGE
WEST SUSSEX

FROM THE SECOND MASTER

12th September, 2009

The Farrington Ward,
Farleigh General Hospital

Dear Roger,

I hope you are well! We are all so sorry to hear about your accident whilst on smoking patrol. I have had a look again at my memorandum concerning staff doing smoking duty, and realise now how easily one could have read "take a minute drag" as "take a minute's drag". Although we sympathise with you for having overdosed on a particularly strong mixture of cannabis and something as yet unidentified by the police, we do hope you will soon be able to look back and see the funny side of the whole incident.

In the meantime, the boy in question has been severely reprimanded by me and the Head, and is due to appear before the County Court in three weeks for possession of illegal substances. The police are particularly grateful to you for having caught him, as they tell us that this could easily have done a great deal of damage to his long-term health, possibly even having to spend months in hospital.

Brian and Barry, from Health and Safety, are looking again at reworking my words, so that in future such announcements cannot in themselves constitute a Health and Safety risk!

Thank-you for all your sterling efforts!

Yours truly,

Peregrine I. Grueson

[54]

Hello, all!
We're all still out here,
just about sane! Hope your term's
going well, and I hope to see you soon.
Not all the pupils have been able to
get their work finished which was
kindly sent out, especially those
who have lost a hand or two, but
please bear with them. We've been
moved a couple of times now, and
are currently somewhere quite
horrific! Still, could be worse, as I
say to my pupils here, all of them are
absolute troopers!

Tim

The Common Room,
St. Cretien's Coll.,
Sedgwickham,
West Sussex,
Inglaterra.

School office memorandum – Common room notice board

Saturday Evening Detentions   12 . 9 . 09

Nobbie Styles	single	playing with a ball in class
Jeffrey Hirst	single	Drama: Rushing lines, "Man Barrow Muff!"
Geoffrey Salad	single	Behaviour
Eleanor Filler	single	Smoking
Priam Hardy	single	Behaviour and inappropriate response
Gillian Querty	single	Smoking
George Humphrey	single	Smoking something illegal
Harry Dercules	single	Smoking something unheard of
Jacqui Charlton	double	Taking a trophy from the House Cupboard
Jennifer Thwaite	single	Smoking in Chemistry
Robert Moore	single	Always insisting on being House Captain
Christopher Robin	double	Fake claims to being on a sponsored silence
Seline Finghumpton	single	Chewing in lessons (twice)
Hyacinthe Redoubt	single	Cycling over the Quad
Trevor Hui-Yang	double	Missing periods 3 & 4, Thursday
Oscar Uncthorpe	single	Smoking in his room
Frederick Sallyhope	single	Certain events on the School Farm
Graham Graham	single	Setting light to incense not in religious context
Vaughan Smiler	double	Indecent attention towards a member of staff
Benjamin Stroke	single	Behaviour towards the new intake
Silas Petticoat	double	Mobile in chapel with v. offensive ring tone

All detentions will take place in **TMM's room** (Science 9) from 7.30 pm till 10.00
Entrance to disco thereafter will be left to House Parent's discretion, case by case.

SATURDAY EVENING
STAFF DUTY PATROL REPORT

Date: *12/9/09*
Duty Team Leader: *Vernon Bottockson*
Duty Team: *ONP, SER*

An awful evening's duty. All far too excited at being back with their mates. Not helped by this week's disco, with a couple of DJs calling themselves the "Ghetto Blasters", whose mix of music was from beginning to end a call to arms and revolution, and whose witty repartee throughout consisted of goading the pupils into "rising up against the oppressor scum." My team (Olivia Power and Samantha Rectoil) felt constantly threatened, and at one point we were barricaded inside the Great Hall, where the disco was being held, and were held down by a "delegation" of Fifth Formers demanding their own common room and coffee machine, else the Headmaster's house would be stormed and set alight. We acquiesced simply to get some fresh air.

Outside, I caught Calvin Groote and Sarah Tithe smoking again, and sent them back to house, but Sarah came out again later, and I caught her in a compromising situation with Paolo Wright in the boys' toilets. After confiscating her bottle of vodka, I sent them both back to House, and alerted the relevant people.

Three boys in the pond at lock-up time; we sent them back to house along with the four pupils on the roof of the squash courts, who were singing "I believe I can fly" by the popular singer R.Kelly. Everyone rather over-excited tonight. Didn't get home until 12.45 God, Saturday night duties are bloody dreadful.

VOB

Oh dear! Sorry you did not have a good night Vernon. Thank-you for all your notes, and I shall action a number of things that have come out of them ready for next week. Onwards and upwards!

Peregrine

COMMON ROOM NOTICE BOARD

The Senior Management Team has decided that in the build-up to the looming TOFFSTED Inspection, there will have to be an over-arching implementation of standardised pupil/staff appraisal, in order to ensure that we are all conforming to an approved set of compliance criteria.

To this end, we have decided to appoint Mr. Thomas Horngold as <u>Inspection Enforcement Officer</u>. Despite his rather aggressive-sounding title, the Enforcement Officer will be acting in a primarily consultative and advisory capacity, and his long-term aim is simply to get us all "singing from the same hymn sheet," by the time the Inspectors arrive in the Summer Term.

At various times over the next two terms, Thomas will be asking to see samples of your pupils' work, in order to look over the standards of marking, and to oversee the way Heads of Department oversee your marking. This is in no way intended to appear threatening, but we would like all staff to cooperate as closely as possible with this process.

Should he need to, Thomas will also be requesting not only one-to-one meetings with all members of staff, but would also like to observe a number of classes, in order to give some constructive feedback to colleagues, should there be any need to, in time for the Inspection proper.

In the meantime, we do hope you will give your undiluted support to Thomas in whatever he needs to do. This would be a tough job for anyone, as there are a large number of ways in which St. Cretien's College is not at all compliant with what will be needed for the inspection, and there are, what's more a number of, let's say, "vested interests" which will need to be ripped out and stamped on for good.

Many thanks to all involved,
(Let's hope we pull through this time.)

Anthony Ingham

Anthony Ingham, Director of Studies

ST. CRETIEN'S COLLEGE

STAFF APPRAISAL

Subject observed: **Geogr.**	Observed by: **P.I.Grueson**
Teacher observed: **B.O. Kuller**	Date: **Mon. 14th Sept, 2009**

Number of pupils: **7: (3 boys, 4 girls)**

Period: **5 + 6**

Year: **Lower Sixth Form**

Lesson aims: **Social effects of the Green Revolution in 1970's**
- enable a basic analysis of scatter graphs
- introduce concept of population pyramid

General comments:

At first, I felt that Barry Kuller would make a great deal of progress with this class, as he had from the outset an atmosphere of quiet calm, even an eerie silence. I have to say I think that Barry did not make the most of this advantage; I personally would very much relish having the kind of peace and quiet I saw in evidence here.

Unfortunately, within only a few minutes, Barry reacted rather badly to a comment made by one of the girls, who had ventured her answer only after numerous and I must say inappropriate threats from Barry. I sat in silence at the back of the class, and perhaps my presence made the class particularly reticent on the day, but in the end Barry, I feel, did over-react to her answer (it was, it turns out, wrong by a year), and he then howled at the seven pupils, banging his clenched fist on their desks, and finally sweeping their books and equipment off their desks, Barry gave each one a couple of sheets of paper, and told them to write lines for the rest of the double lesson. The phrase, "I must not stoop to the level of an intellectual pygmy when answering questions in front of Mr. Grueson" I deemed was also inappropriate and irrelevant.

I spoke to Barry at the end of the lesson to ask him how he felt it had gone, and he admitted that he had not been able to follow the lesson plan as closely as he would have liked, and accepted that he may have over-reacted to Amelia's wrong answer. However, on the plus side, he did feel that he had kept control of a situation in which he has often allowed his emotions to get the better of him.

I have recommended to him a course in London next month on class management and hope he will get plenty out of this. I do feel that Barry has plenty to offer as a first class teacher, but that sometimes his reactions to events can be to the detriment of his pupils.

Peregrine I. Grueson

ST. CRETIEN'S COLLEGE
STAFF APPRAISAL

Subject observed: **French**	Observed by: **P.I.G.**
Teacher observed: **H. Pukeman**	Date: **15. 09. 09**

Number of pupils: **21 Fifth Formers**

Period: **4**

Lesson aims: To develop the pupils' ability to use bilingual dictionaries, and to highlight the pitfalls of over- or misuse. By the end, pupils should be able to look up certain definitions and

General comments: explain what they found.

Henry began well, talking individually to pupils as they came in, giving back their prep, and highlighting what he had marked. Looking at a number of pupils' books, I felt that comments could do with being longer, grades should be seen to be more consistently linked with the agreed template for school marking, and Henry's own handwriting was not always totally legible; he should work more on his "d"s and "q"s.

In the lesson itself, Henry engaged well with the pupils, who listened attentively for the most part, and though he did try to impress upon them not to call out answers, I feel that, rather than just telling them so, he should have perhaps empowered the children to come to that conclusion through a more democratic, child-centred debate.

I should like to know how Henry chooses which pupil to select for answering a question; I saw no evidence of a systematic distribution of selection, and my own rough calculation based on this observation suggests that he primarily chose pupils from the far side left hand quadrant, by a fraction. I have recommended to him at the very least his attending a course on even-handedness next month in London, but he should certainly be paying more attention to this on a more regular basis, as it can lead to such disillusionment among the pupils.

Although Henry did cover what he needed to with the dictionary work, his five-minute filler at the end was hardly related to what had just been done, and I wonder whether this was of any real value to the class? Although the pupils clearly enjoyed the language game, did it really cement the body of work done today? Also, too much competitiveness is not to be encouraged in children. Otherwise, a very good lesson, as much for Henry as the pupils. Well done !

Peregrine I. Grueson

ST. CRETIEN'S COLLEGE
STAFF APPRAISAL

Subject observed: *French*	Observed by: *RHP*
Teacher observed: *HGPukeman*	Date: 18 / 9 / 09

Number of pupils: 17

Period: 1

Lesson aims: *Introducing telling the time, revision of numbers, etc*

General comments: *Fine*

Reginald

ST. CRETIEN'S COLLEGE
STAFF APPRAISAL

Subject observed: **Biology**	Observed by: **P.I.G.**
Teacher observed: **Sonja Mangle**	Date: **18. 09. 09**

Number of pupils: **24 Third Formers**

Period: **2**

Lesson aims: To introduce the topic of Human Reproduction and look at outdated ideas of genetic/racial contamination

General comments:

I was certainly looking forward to observing this lesson, and seeing how Sonja treated this sensitive subject with the Third Form. I must say that I thought she did a sterling job of examining their previous preps, and then highlighting some of their general failings to the class as a whole. However, I did feel somewhat uncomfortable when she ended up screaming so hard that some of the boys on the front row started to cry, and a girl at the back had to be taken off to the toilet because of a little accident. However, she made her point admirably.

Sonja then began describing the sexual act in consummate detail, which I suppose is how one has to do such things, though I even found myself wincing at some of the points she made. I do wonder whether some of our younger pupils might not be better off exploring some of these topics later in the year. They did all look rather shocked, and I couldn't help noticing how many of them were very subdued, and constantly looked over at me; my presence clearly must have been putting a dampener on what I presume to be a normally bouncy class.

Everyone seemed to get plenty out of Sonja's practical demonstrations of certain contraceptives, and then took lots of notes from the board. As I went round to examine their work, I was most impressed by the neatness of it all, except for one very troubled little boy who had started to scribble frantically things like "Help us" and "Get us out of this hell". When this was pointed out, Sonja very gently took him off to what she calls her "Cool-off Cupboard", and the class quickly settled down again.

Not entirely sure I agree with some of the areas Sonja explored, especially the potential contamination of certain races through unprotected sex, and the references to maintaining the purity of our blood against racial bacilli. Still, the pupils were clearly enthralled, and they certainly learned a great deal of useful stuff which will be so important to them later. Well done!

Peregrine I. Grueson

ST. CRETIEN'S COLLEGE
WEST SUSSEX

FROM THE SECOND MASTER

19th September, 2009

To: Head of Biology

Re: The role of religion in biology lessons

Dear Salvador,

It was brought to my attention by a colleague in your own department that certain aspects of your religious views have recently impinged somewhat on your professional approach to the subject. I refer, of course, to your strong (and admirable) faith in the Scientologist version of events, and your sterling determination to incorporate the literal interpretation of this set of beliefs into your teaching of Biology.

Having consulted with the other members of the SMT, I feel that we ought perhaps to have a frank and open discussion with you on this subject, not least because an A-level pupil was worried enough to talk to another member of your department about one of your recent lessons on Darwin, which he alleges culminated in your burning a copy of the Origin of Species.

Please pop in to talk further with me.

Thanks. Yours in no way judgmentally or closed-mindedly,

Peregrine I. Grueson

19/09/09: PIG

School office memorandum – Common room notice board

Saturday Evening Detentions   19 . 9 . 09

Timothy Taylor	single	Claiming to be a landlord
Fuller Young	double	Being overly proud of coming from the capital
Wadworth Jennings	single	Filling his language with six-letter expletives
Simon Pilfer	double	Theft
Geoffrey Salad	single	Smoking
Gillian Querty	single	Smoking
Marr Stones	single	Going on about the old empire
Duke Errs	double	Over-egging his Scottishness
Veronica Hulk	single	Smoking and blowing rings in German
Seline Finghumpton	single	Chewing in lessons (three times)
Priam Hardy	single	Incident which left whole art class traumatised
Adnam Badger	single	Getting feet tangled on Broad Side
Oscar Uncthorpe	single	Smoking in bath in Boarding House
Frederick Sallyhope	single	More misbehaviour on the School Farm
Naomi Shepherd	single	Habitually spitting into fireplaces
Trevor Hui-Yang	double	Missing periods 5 & 6, Wednesday
Graham Graham	single	Blaming Chapel for his own shortcomings
Vaughan Smiler	double	Uninvited appearance at member of staff's flat
Austell Sharpes	single	Being full of doom (bar-humbug)
Benjamin Stroke	single	Behaviour towards new intake
Theo Waites	double	Being too northern and bluff
Trent Chang	double	Knowing more about China than his teacher

All detentions will take place in **TMM's room** (Science 9) from 7.30 pm till 10.00
Entrance to disco thereafter will be left to house parent's discretion, case by case.

THE ST. CRETIEN'S

DEBATING SOCIETY

Please join us in the Library for this week's debate,
followed by tea, coffee and biscuits

This week's motion:

THIS HOUSE BELIEVES THAT COMMUNITY SERVICE MERELY ENCOURAGES THE HELPLESS

*

Thursday, 7.30 pm

Please ensure you obtain your Housemaster's / Housemistress'
permission beforehand

Memo: From MAS

DATE: 21/9/09 **RE:** Prize-Giving Ceremony concerns

Peregrine,

I am writing confidentially to you with the intention of putting down a few thoughts I had regarding yesterday's prize-giving ceremony. I admit to having a number of concerns about what happened, and I just feel I should convey them in writing to you, openly and honestly.

Whilst I think it was an excellent idea to hold the ceremony in conjunction with the Sesquicentennial Celebrations, after its unfortunate cancellation last term, I do wonder, first and foremost, whether it needed to last three-and-a-half hours, especially coming after the Chaplain's sermon in the service, which he very cleverly timed to last for exactly 150 minutes, God bless him.

This was not helped, either, by the choice of music which interspersed the whole event. Did we have to hear the juniors singing and miming to their awful version of *Kumbayah My Lord*, or indeed later the seniors with their full-on version of *Anarchy in the UK*, complete with spitting into the assembled audience of parents and pupils. I noticed a real fear spread palpably amongst some of our parents, even as little Damien Pondboy sang the words, "I am the Antichrist..." and some of the juniors were in floods of tears by the end of it all. Equally inappropriate, I felt, was to finish with Toby Standard on the tuba, playing all eight verses of My Grandfather's Clock — at least this cheered people up, though, with, thankfully, tears of laughter by the end of the tortuous last verse.

As to the prizes themselves, I wonder whether some of these prizes aren't just a little out-of-tune with what a modern school should be giving; some of them are indeed downright divisive. Ones to be considered, surely, are the prizes for: Nicest Boy/Nicest Girl; Best Looking Pupil; Most Improved Looks through Puberty; Overcoming Personality Adversity; Best All-Rounder; Most Teachable; Most Surprising Results; Funniest Boy/Funniest Girl.

I was also surprised by the behaviour of the Guest Presenter, Mr. Giles Hurler, Head Master of Gatchwick Prep School. It seemed to me that he was perfectly fine shaking the boys' hands each time they came up for a prize, but with the girls he was downright creepy. Did he need to kiss them (rather slobbily, I later learned) on both cheeks and then pat them on the behind, before giving each one their prize with a lingering handshake? With Emily Bounteous from the Upper Sixth, he visibly dribbled, and nearly swallowed her whole head. Maybe not one to invite next year?

As for the speech by the Chair of the Governors... Why on earth did he think it appropriate to expound on his personal theories on the links between the financial crisis and sexual permissiveness? The pupils were either bored or utterly fascinated, and our parents were rightly uncomfortable. Following this with a "xylophone gala" was also quite surreal.

I hope you don't mind my sharing these concerns with you.

Yours,

Michael Storr

THE CHAPLAINCY
St. Cretien's College

A transcript of the Extraordinary Prayer to Mark the School's Sesquicentennial Anniversary, as used in yesterday's Special School Chapel Service:

> O LORD, who hast blessed this SCHOOL with such fecundity,
> We pray now that THOU bringest unto this place
> Such guidance as we shall surely need to face the future
> And to help us brave the difficulties to come.
>
> Show us how we should ensure that ST. CRETIEN'S persists in its good works
> For the next one-hundred-and-fifty years, and the next after those;
> Let the SCHOOL shine as a beacon to the world,
> Let us radiate our brilliance even unto the darkest shores of other lands,
> Giving aid and succour to the poor and destitute,
> And let the press write about it this year with more vigour than last.
>
> Give us the knowledge to understand what is right,
> And open our eyes to the truth,
> Especially in what is told unto us by those who lead us;
> And open their eyes too, for they oftentimes do not see the wood for the trees,
> And help them to see when they are wrong or misguided,
> Above all in their allocation of funds to the Chaplaincy.
>
> LORD, guide our pupils in this place as they aspire to become good people,
> And show them the way to behave, unto one another,
> And not be caught in acts of indecency or lewdness,
> For none shall be merciful to beastliness, and they that are so
> Should be SMITTEN down in wrath and righteous fury.
>
> LORD, we pray that you look after all those in our flock who have strayed;
> Be a guide for those who have left but still give no donations;
> Be a guide for those staff who have gone on to better-paid positions;
> For the pupils who come to Sunday services with hangovers;
> For those who last week were swept out to sea in the papier-maché balloons.
>
> O LORD, hear this prayer, and help our School to thrive and prosper
> And BE with us always in our HEARTS and in our TROUGHS. AMEN

© The Senior Chaplain   DIC : 22 / 9 / 09

WELTING HOUSE

Mr. Barry Kuller

Peregrine,

      I am referring this case to you in your capacity as Second Master, and I hope you will be able to deal with the situation in an appropriate manner, as the pupil in question seems not recognise my authority as his House Master *in loco parentis*. I do feel very strongly indeed that he needs to be seen by somebody higher up, and also that he needs to know how seriously I take the principle behind the whole matter.

      It may strike you that the deed in question is of a rather petty nature, and I grant that of itself being caught with extra toiletries in his shower area is probably not as serious as other misdemeanours you must have to deal with. However, as the boy knows perfectly well, I do not allow more than just one tube of shower gel and one shampoo per boy in the shower areas, for all manner of reasons; all the boys in Welting House are aware of the rules I have here, and know that I insist on their abiding by the House rules, regardless of what they claim goes on in other houses.

      Not only did Samuel have a newly bought shower gel already in his area, but when I approached him about this, and confiscated it, he responded inappropriately, and even asked for it back at one point. At every stage of the next few minutes, the boy exacerbated the situation he was already in, until I furiously told him I would be pushing for him to be suspended, even expelled, if he continued.

      Naturally, this is not necessarily the ultimate course I would like to take over a single tube of gel, but I would still appreciate your having a word with him, and perhaps in giving him a double disciplinary detention you might remind him how lucky he is not to have been expelled.

      Thank-you for your efforts in this. The offending item is currently in my study ready to given back to him just as soon as I receive a letter of apology.

Cheers!

Barry

The Master's Lodge,
Sedgwickham,
West Sussex,

28th September, 2009

To all staff

Re: Commemorative Mural Created by the girls in Grilling House

It is with some reluctance that I put this notice out to you all, but I do feel it is worth drawing your attention to what might just be a heinous attempt on the part of some girls to undermine everything that these wonderful Sesquicentennial events represent.

During a number of (frankly interminable) meetings in the Meaddings Hall, ranging from the Pupils' Council through to a recent Staff Pay Committee discussion, I have had the opportunity to look in some detail at the huge mural presented to me and to the school. And I have to say I am a little bit concerned by some of what I think I can see in it.

Is it just me, I wonder, do I have a dirty mind; or is it not possible to discern a number of downright upsetting images hidden within the painting? I refer to the bottom left-hand corner, where I can distinctly see two human-shaped figures doing something unmentionable to one another. In another place, near the top, there is most definitely something bestial (in all senses) happening where the cherry blossom is supposed to be overhanging the tunnel-entrance.

I raise all this chiefly because the act of doing and presenting this mural, ostensibly based on the life of St. Francis, was presumed to have been done in the spirit in which it was received. However, if there was an attempt on the part of Sirene Tremulous-Bayle, the House Captain of Grilling, and her team, to slip something obnoxious past all the staff, then this must be punished. And if any parents spot the hidden details, or even worse, if word gets round, then we shall be a laughing stock. It is not as if I am particularly prudish myself, quite the contrary; but I do worry about the principle of the whole thing, and I am certainly not keen to have been made a fool of, by accepting this work in good faith, when it was in fact gross pornography, sitting there literally stinking right under my very nose.

If any staff cannot see the details to which I am referring, I would be very happy to take them round to the mural and to point them out, preferably when there are no pupils around – we don't want them laughing at us trying to spot things, do we. I also wonder if there are any other hidden features in the piece. Please could all staff spend some time nonchalantly in Meaddings Hall, over the next few days, to see if you can spot any more obscenities.

Many thanks for your efforts with this, as I would certainly like to get to the bottom of it

A. K. Warble

<u>ALL SCHOOL ATTENDANCE</u>

TOMORROW IS THE BIG DAY!!

ST. CRETIEN'S PROCESSION TO VILLAGE GREEN SEDGWICKHAM

Please make sure you are wearing correct school uniform, brush your hair, clean your teeth and polish your shoes.

**Assemble promptly
in front of the Chapel at <u>10:00</u>
and be ready to depart by <u>11:30</u>**

Stay in your positions within your individual Houses, as directed by your House Parent, and remember to be on your best behaviour, as you will very much be ambassadors for your school.

2. 10. 09: PIG

MEMORANDUM from the Second Master

DATE: 4 :9 :09 **RE:** Sesquicentennial celebrations

Let me begin on a positive note. There are some positive notes.

On the whole, we have to admit that these two weeks of celebrations and events have been an extremely uplifting experience, bringing the school together in ways we have not seen in a long time. In large part, that is thanks to you, the staff, for all you help in organising and supervising the various activities that have gone on.

However, there are certainly a few lessons to be learned. Let's start with the less toxic issues first, though toxicity is perhaps the point concerning the tree-painting project. Our groundstaff tell me it will take years, maybe even decades for some of the trees to recover, and that it was an altogether careless idea to paint the tree-trunks, and in some cases all the leaves of St. Cretien's tree population with industrial-grade gloss and emulsion, however pretty it looked. Unfortunately, not everybody thought it looked very pretty, either...

The case of the elderly lady found in the toilets after dark, having been left there after one of Glibb House's outreach projects must never be repeated.

It was unfortunate that David Swelling was put in charge of organising the route for the procession to Sedgwickham, given his track record on the cross-country route. However, it is a pity that people think me to be so inflexible with regard to Health and Safety issues, that they did not try to change the route back, even without an authorized Risk Assessment in place – we were lucky not to have had any serious accidents on both times we crossed the A2472.

Nor was the whole affair helped by those staff who took the idea of going to the Hare and Hounds a little too literally. This did not help matters at all.

Perhaps the less said about last night's extravaganza the better, at least until the fire brigade has filed its full report. Suffice it to say, that we really cannot afford to have any more gas leaks. In view of the awfulness of what might have happened, we can only say again how lucky St. Cretien's seems to be.

School's festival a real blast!

There was shock this weekend at the prestigious fee-paying independent school St. Cretien's College, when what was supposed to be a grand climax to a fortnight's festivities came to a shuddering, near-fatal jolt, writes **Ellie Hopes**, for the Sedgwickham Herald

At the end of a day of high pomp and circumstance, during which the entire school processed out of its gates and across the fields to the centre of Sedgwickham, the pupils and staff were supposed to enjoy a bonfire and an informal party with fireworks.

However, due to a number of "technical glitches," terrified onlookers were subjected to a horrific spectacle which threatened to set the whole school ablaze.

One witness, Mr. Henry Pukeman, a teacher at the £16,500-a-year private school, said, "It was one of the most eye-watering fireworks displays I have ever seen. I couldn't see properly for about an hour afterwards."

The day had not got off to a good start, either, as the route the school had chosen to take into the village trespassed over private land, and crossed the A2472 bypass at a point of particularly bad visibility. Thankfully, nobody was injured, but traffic on the busy dual-carriageway came to a standstill in both directions for forty-five minutes, and again later, as the school returned after the ceremony.

But it was the events that took place in the evening that shook the whole school, and resulted in ten fire crews being called out to St. Cretien's for the sixth time this year.

Alongside a traditional hog-roast, set up underneath one of the boarding houses, a number of the pupils had organised a grand display of fireworks, to mark the 150th anniversary of the school's foundation. These were to be set off, supervised by English teacher Dr. Roger Pampo, from the roof of the boarding house, at around 7pm, at the close of the event.

Unfortunately, the hog-roast proved to be a much more intense fire than expected, with, according to some eyewitnesses, flames reaching up to 150ft. The heat then generated is what fire fighters believe caused the fireworks to go off in such a spectacular manner, and fire officers sifting through the debris the next day said that, once the hog-roast had reached the roof, there was no way that the fireworks could be let off in a controlled manner. This, coupled with a localised gas leak, created a massive fireball, which enveloped the whole quad.

Within 30 seconds, all 150 fireworks had exploded, some of them taking off in unexpected directions, given that Dr. Pampo was still in the process of setting them up. The result was described by some onlookers as the most incredible fireworks display they had ever seen.

This latest scare comes in the wake of a largely controversial fortnight of ceremonies. OAPs in Sedgwickham have described being "ripped off" by pupils ostensibly doing "good deeds." In one case, pensioner Harry Trefoil (69) had his entire front garden crazy-paved against his will, and Winnifred Bene (78) was brought into the school for an organised lunch, only to be forgotten and inexplicably left in the boys' toilets.

Furthermore, a mural specially painted by pupils for the Head was found to contain images of a sexual nature, which have shocked staff and parents. No-one was available today to comment.

ST. CRETIEN'S COLLEGE
WEST SUSSEX

FROM THE SECOND MASTER

5th October, 2009

The Farrington Ward,
Farleigh General Hospital

Dear Roger,

I hope I find you well, now! I must say, you weren't looking as bad as we thought you might, as we dragged you down from the roof, and in conversation with your consultant, I understand that it was primarily the shock of it all that caused the reaction you had. I must say, you had everyone quite worried indeed at the time!

We are all delighted to know that you'll be back on board the good ship HMS St. Cretien's within the month, and we look forward to having you around again. In the meantime, do not spare a single thought for your classes, as we were lucky enough to be able to employ Mrs. Eileen Gerryband again, who covered your absence last month, after your unfortunate inhaling incident! She wants me to let you know that the classes will be in very safe hands till you come back, as she is becoming quite familiar with the pupils and their needs, now, not least due to her stint last year, when she covered you after the bank-robbery incident.

If it's any consolation at all, everyone who witnessed the fireworks going off has said that it was really one of the most impressive events they have ever attended, and were so glad they were there to see it. The ones who enjoyed it the most said that the spectacle was seen to its best advantage from behind the Main Hall and the other side of the Jeville Lawns, but even those in the thick of it say it was something they'll find hard to forget.

You may also be interested to know that the main cause for the explosion was in fact another gas leak, which had been building up from somewhere near the Boarding House, which fire investigators are still looking into. But, basically, you do not need to worry about the accusations that were flying around on the night, or the threats of legal action levelled against you as you were put into the ambulance. These have all been dropped now.

Brian and Barry, from Health and Safety, are looking again at the measures in place for such events, but say there is little they can do to improve such events when so many factors are in play.

Thank-you again, Roger, for all your sterling efforts!

Yours truly,

Peregrine I. Grueson

MEMORANDUM from the Second Master

DATE: 05 :10 :09   **RE:**   The Gas Situation

To all staff,

As you know, the little problem of gas leaking on site has reared its ugly head again, and overnight, we have had to implement a number of quite intrusive measures to the school site, beginning with the complete shutting-down of the entire gas system.

You will also have noticed the appearance of temporary shower units in front of every Boarding House. These have been necessary, if the school is to function for the next few weeks, so that the pupils have access to hot water and sanitation facilities.

Last night, Priam Hardy, of course, was the first boy to try using the girls' shower unit, claiming that his own House's was full, and that he was desperate to "wash away all dirty thoughts." Naturally, he claimed not to have seen anything he shouldn't, as he was wearing some kind of blindfold. Bizarrely, this was made from a pair of ladies' tights, beggaring the question of where he acquired these?!! He has been severely reprimanded, and will serve a detention this weekend.

We really don't want the press getting wind of any of this again, so please do refrain from talking too loudly about it to friends from outside the school or down the pub (for the benefit of those young masters who frequent such watering holes). Therefore, in emails around the school, please refer to this issue only with the codename: "*MASSIVE GAS LEAK*"

Thank-you for your sensitivity and discretion in this matter,

Peregrine

05. 10. 09: PIG

X-ViruChekked: Checked
From: Hip@stcretiens.org.uk
Date: Tue, 7 Oct 2009 13:54:43 EST
Subject: A funny place
To: royandbrenda@yahoo.co.uk
X-Mailer: CompuServ 2001 6.0 for Windeyes UK sub 233309
X-MD-d: royandbrenda@yahoo.co.uk X-Return-Path:
hip@school@stcretiens.org.uk
Reply-To: hip@school@stcretiens.org.uk

Mum and Dad,

Hi! It has been an extraordinary week of events, and it just seems to get better and better here.

First of all, the procession to the local village of Sedgwickham had been billed as a grand, solemn march to the very place where our beloved founder had started his teaching career. Well, to get there, after being shouted at by a farmer who wanted us out of his crops, we then had to cross four lanes of fast moving traffic, and it was only thanks to a pupil's brilliant idea of letting some sheep out from an adjacent field onto the tarmac, that we were were able to slow the traffic down enough for us all to make a run for it.

When we got to the place where a memorial was to be unveiled, it was, of course, the local Hare and Hounds public house! Not only did the entire school of 550 pupils, 60-odd staff plus caterers, matrons and cleaners all stand right in front of it, blocking the way in and out for users of the pub, for a whole hour and a half, but the Head kept on going on about abstinence, temperance and the dangers of alcohol dependency.

Then a plaque was unveiled, half way up the wall, in which St. Cretien's was spelled without the second "e" and the description of our founder came across downright creepy, compounded by the phrase "hard shaft" instead of "hard graft". We finished with a rousing version of our new school hymn, which had to end after only two verses, due to booing from inside the pub and down the street.

Some of that booing came from colleagues of mine, who had decided to sneak into the pub, which meant that, after 1 ½ hours drinking, they were in no fit state to accompany the school back over the bypass and across private land (this time we were met with shots fired over our heads to ward us off! To no avail – the school marched solemnly on!).

In the evening, a perfect storm of hog-roast, fireworks and a gas leak resulted in such a spectacular show that you will no doubt have read all about it in the newspapers. Needless to say, it was yet another horror show from St. Cretien's, somehow avoiding any major injuries, again! The result is complete closure of our gas supply and a line of awful temporary shower units attached to the boarding houses – no such luxury for the staff, though, who have to make do with cold showers!

with much love,

Henry

The St. Cretien's

Christian
Union

is meetin' next thurs

7.30pm
in the
Chapel Crypt

Subject: "**just** who *the* **hell**

does JESUS think *he is*

?!"

Yo, be there peeps!!

School office memorandum – Common room notice board

Saturday Evening Detentions   10 . 10 . 09

Sophie Phucouite	single	Smoking
Eleanor Filler	single	Smoking
Damien Pondboy	single	Arrogant ignorance
Gillian Querty	single	Smoking
Trevor Hui-Yang	double	Missing periods 1 & 2, Monday
Bella Yowler	single	Uniformed infringed – & no fishnets allowed
William Vellicose	single	Smiling inappropriately at prospective parents
Jennifer Thwaite	single	Smoking something utterly shocking
Priam Hardy	double	Using the girls' shower unit poorly blindfolded
Oscar Uncthorpe	single	Smoking in showers
Frederick Sallyhope	single	Inappropriate incident on the School Farm
Graham Graham	single	Undermining early morning chapel
Vaughan Smiler	double	Stalking staff at weekend in Sainsbury's
Benjamin Stroke	double	Behaviour towards juniors
Harvey Hunksnare	single	Tiring out his teacher with endless chat
Guthry Cull	single	Making up words to confuse cover teacher
Seymour Schiedt	single	Over-egging the pudding in Home Economics
Theo Rectulum	double	Showing things off which shouldn't be shown
Sirene Tremulous-Bayle	double	Putting obscene elements into the Head's Mural
Guthrie Force-Banner	single	Adding blue colouring to the cantine pasta
Bella O'Nyons	double	Hiding in a tumble-dryer before bedtime
Ariadne Wesley-Jones	single	Thinking she was being funny in early Chapel

All detentions will take place in **TMM's room** (Science 9) from 7.30 pm till 10.00
Entrance to disco thereafter will be left to house parent's discretion, case by case.

SATURDAY EVENING
STAFF DUTY PATROL REPORT

Date: *10/10/09*
Duty Team Leader: *Frank Thorney*
Duty Team: *PWB, TPS*

Appalling behaviour all round. Chasing too many pupils out of smoking areas, but to no avail. Even started to offer us cigarettes and alcohol, in exchange for not being reported! Unbelievable...

Patricia failed to persuade one group of Fifth Formers to move away from the staff flats behind Harding Quad, and they claimed their human rights were being infringed. When Terence and I came to support her, we were treated to such vitriol that Patricia fainted, and didn't come out of the staff bar, where we had been obliged to force a brandy or two down her (at the school's expense, I might add, Peregrine, unless you wish to take personal responsibility for some of the discipline here at St. Cretien's).

As I am still quite new, I could not name all the pupils involved, and took down copious names of boys and girls, who in fact did not exist, or had left the school two or three years ago. It was not until I was being fed such names as Nina Simone, Kurt Cobain, Frank Sinatra, Perry Como and Diego Maradonna that I realised just how barefaced and devious some of the children here are.

Finished flushing out the last of the smokers and drinkers at around 1.00am. Hope this is not the norm for a Saturday night at St. Cretien's...

FAT

Oh dear! Sounds like you did have a rather tough night Frank !! I can assure you that St. Cretien's is not always as bad as this, and yes, I do take my responsibilities here very seriously indeed as regards the discipline. Please do put those brandies on my bar account. I shall action a number of points that have arisen from your constructive criticism.

Peregrine

ST. CRETIEN'S COLLEGE
WEST SUSSEX

FROM THE SECOND MASTER

Second Master's Lodge,

Sunday, 1st November, 2009

Dear Parents and Guardians,
As we approach the beginning of the second half of Michaelmas Term, I feel this is an appropriate occasion to remind you of some of our most fundamental rules concerning the comportment of your children here in a boarding school. I hope you will understand the importance of these rules which effectively contribute to the successful functioning of such a community as St. Cretien's.

First and foremost, following recent incidents, and especially as your child will soon be returning to school with all his or her heart desires in terms of home comforts, I must emphasise now that absolutely no pets are allowed to be kept in the pupils' studies or indeed on the school premises. This is not only understandably for the benefit of our cleaning staff (the unfortunate case of a Vietnamese pot-bellied pig smuggled into and kept permanently in a pupil's study resulted last month in the loss of five valued members of our cleaning staff); but it is also for the sake of the animals themselves, which are often unsuited to the unnatural environment of a teenager's bedroom, and die, as was the case with the kittens last Summer Term. The fact that the girl responsible for their inexcusable deaths was severely traumatised by the occurrence, and hid all eight of them behind her bed until mid July merely adds to stress for all of us in this whole, unfortunate business of bringing pets into school.

As if this needs any further emphasis, recent events involving animals escaping has added to our concern. Whilst some survive (and it is true that the trees behind Hythe House have indeed been enlivened thanks to the establishment of a successful colony of budgerigars after a fad for these pets amongst the boys there), others are less likely to survive, and the tragic death of a tortoise last week crossing the school drive is a typical story, whilst others are simply more difficult to track down.

Without wishing to alarm parents or pupils, for instance, we have yet to locate Timmy the Tarantula, which escaped about three weeks ago, and repeated sightings by hysterical pupils and staff indicate that he is surviving perfectly well in the rafters of our old boarding houses. But as I say, we are working very hard with exotic animal experts, and there really is no cause for concern!

Pets are proving to be not the only problem. Music systems are also increasingly a nuisance at St. Cretien's, and in studies which command a view over public places such as the Quad, I would urge pupils not to continue to vie with one another to impose their own particular tastes on everybody else who lives on or walks through those parts of the school. Most upsetting of all for the reputation of St. Cretien's was a police armed unit swoop at gone midnight last week in response to complaints from the nearby village of St. Withers about an imagined illegal rave. This turned out to be one Fifth Former, blasting out music from his new hi-fi system. Chief Constable Evelyn Hall also commented that the aerials some boys have constructed now interfere with police transmissions frequencies, so I hope that there will be no repeat of this.

I am afraid to say I was also disappointed at the way that certain aspects of our grand Sesquicentennial (150th) Anniversary celebrations were turned into underhand ways to undermine the school and the staff who work so hard here. I am referring, of course, to the discovery that the Time Capsule that Deeping House buried five feet under the Back Terrace (at great expense, I might add) contained a number of sets of keys belonging to teaching staff, as well as other items. This kind of behaviour completely undoes all the good work a school like St. Cretien's does, especially at a time when so many things were deserving of praise. This kind of thoughtless prank, however, does nothing to help Dr. Tongle, who bought a new car because he thought he'd lost his keys; nor does it comfort Mr. Powte, who thought he'd lost all his classes' coursework, and felt he had to make up the scores (again). As for drugging Mr. Tidy's cat, and putting the poor thing down there, this was a simply unforgiveable act, and one which I imagine our descendants might well have judged us on, regarding our moral rectitude. I can only say I was glad she woke up in time to screech at the pupils all singing *In The Year 2525* around it.

Finally, the thorny question of tuck once again. May I take this opportunity to remind you that the school takes very seriously indeed its responsibility to provide three wholesome meals per day for each and every pupil, and that, regardless of inevitable bouts of teenage dislike for Dining Hall dinners, the boys and girls at St. Cretien's should treat these meals as their primary source of nutrition. A limited and reasonable amount of tuck may be brought into the school, of course, but the school would like to see no repetition of last month's excesses, with some pupils actually converting their shared rooms into an alternative canteen, resulting in poor hygiene and fourteen cases of food-poisoning, whilst another boy brought back so much food that he did not emerge from his room for a week and a half, and was only discovered when animals on the school farm he managed began to die of malnutrition.

I hope you will accept these thoughts in the manner in which they were intended, as useful, valuable advice and guidelines appropriately articulated for the efficient and successful running of a twenty-first century boarding school.

Thank-you very much indeed for your time and cooperation.

Yours sincerely,

Peregrine I. Grueson

1/11/09: PIG

Dr. Titus
Tongle

"A UNIQUE OPPORTUNITY" FOR ALL AGES!!!

Fräulein **MANGLE** IS RUNNING AN INFORMAL

WELDING WORKSHOP

ALL WELCOME, ROOM 13
THURSDAY 4.00

BIOLOGY DEPARTM.,
SC.BUILDG

no specialist equipment needed. just young, healthy bodies!

snm

THE ST. CRETIEN'S

DEBATING SOCIETY

Please join us in the Library for this week's debate,
followed by tea, coffee and biscuits

This week's motion:

THIS HOUSE BELIEVES THAT FASHION IS THE VAIN ATTEMPT TO HIDE CANKEROUS UGLINESS

*

Thursday, 7.30 pm

Please ensure you obtain your Housemaster's / Housemistress'
permission beforehand

School office memorandum – Common room notice board

<u>Saturday Evening Detentions</u>   7 . 11 . 09

Dave Ross	single	Creating a whole army of robots in Metalwork
Tim Lords	single	Wandering for long time without permission
Priam Hardy	single	Setting traps for staff
Eleanor Filler	single	Smoking
Kerry Wedge	single	Filling school fountain with washing up liquid
Darrel Hicks	double	Threatening to take over the universe
Sally Drippe	single	Pining too much for lost love
Seline Finghumpton	single	Chewing in lessons (thrice)
Si Bermen	single	Insisting on there being a 10th planet in Science
Trevor Hui-Yang	double	Missing periods 3 & 4, Tuesday
Gayle Fray	single	Overly judgmental on her fellow housemates
Vaughan Smiler	double	Visiting staff at inappropriate times
Graham Graham	single	Rallying atheists to his denunciation of Chapel
Oscar Uncthorpe	single	Smoking in bed
Silas Petticoat	double	Mobile phone in chapel & v. offensive ring tone
Frederick Sallyhope	single	Indecent treatment of school pigs
Weng-Chiang O'Mega	single	Impersonating a stereotypical oriental tyrant
Christopher Robin	double	Fake claims to being on a sponsored silence
Henry Cnut-Fowler	single	Wheezing loudly throughout Head's Assembly
Grendel Master	double	Causing all manner of problems
Reginald Bolleck	single	Sighing constantly throughout Chapel
Belinda Gutter	double	Pretending to be trapped in her room

All detentions will take place in **TMM's room** (Science 9) from 7.30 pm till 10.00
Entrance to disco thereafter will be left to house parent's discretion, case by case.

Revd. Caustick - Chaplain

THE CHAPLAINCY
St. Cretien's College

To all House Masters,

I would like to ask you all for your assistance in eliminating some of the more loutish behaviour amongst our pupils in Chapel. I do feel really rather strongly that in recent weeks, our boys and girls have done precious little to endear themselves to the Good Lord in His House, let alone to me or any of my Assistant Clergy!! Please would you take the trouble in Chapel this coming Sunday evening to keep a close eye on who exactly is causing trouble in the congregation, and let me know, as well as dealing with it in House.

In particular this last Sunday, I found it rather tedious indeed that there was a widespread playing of the J-game, whereby members of the congregation coughed loudly each time they heard a word starting with "J." It was especially irritating this week, given that our visiting preacher, the Revd. Justin Jones, began first by introducing himself, then giving the title of his sermon, "Jerusalem, Judea, and the jarring juxtaposition of Jesus and Jewish jokes." Our pupils clearly thought manna had fallen from Heaven.

I wonder if you could all try to stem the tide of this lack of respect amongst the more senior of your charges. Thank-you.

The Senior Chaplain

8 / 11 / 09

DIC : 8.11.09

MEMORANDUM from the Second Master

DATE: 9 :11 :09

The following pupils have been suspended:

Dudley Brackwasher	Deeping House
Sally Willershins	Grilling House

- for inappropriate behaviour at the weekend. Their parents will also be asked to contribute to costs to repair the photocopier.
- they will return after Leave Weekend

Frederick Sanjit	Welting House
Drew Heller	Dreer House
Gareth Rowling-Smythers	Dreer House

- for selling illegal substances to juniors. They will also be expected to visit Darren Copes (3rd Form) in the Infirmary at least twice a week, once they return after Leave Weekend

Byron Hunker	Welting House
Ferdinand Wales-Guthrie	Scanker's House

- for convincing their Matron over a period of several weeks that some of the juniors were chronic bed wetters
- for using their own urine as evidence of this
- they will return after Leave Weekend, and their parents will be paying for new mattresses in Scanker's and Welting junior dormitories

9. 11. 09: PIG

10th November, 2009
Welting House

The Head Master,
St. Cretien's School,
West Sussex

Dear Mr. Warble,

Thank-you very much for the chat last week, and for all the encouragement. As I said at the time, I am indeed thoroughly enjoying myself here at St. Cretien's, and hope that my pupils are having as much fun as I am! And, yes, I am making a lot of new friends here amongst the staff; they are a very engaging crowd!

I am also writing specifically to confirm, having spoken again to Peregrine, that I should very much like to set up a weekly Young Entrepreneurs Club or such like, within the scope of the extra-curricular activities here. If there is enough interest, this could easily turn into something more frequent, but I would like to see how it proceeds first. I shall put up a poster to advertise the club when we come back in Lent Term, ready to start then.

As yet, I have no firm plans as to how the pupils should invest, though the first few sessions will certainly be more theoretical than anything. However, the Bursar has agreed to release a small budget for me, in order to give the pupils a sense of how it feels to be investing and speculating for real, and I am very grateful indeed to him for this. I should add again that I am merely an amateur and a novice at all this, and I trust that my own enthusiasm and little bit of experience might rub off onto the pupils, and fire them up!

I am certainly looking forward to implementing some of my theories regarding the way the financial situation is developing and the similarities between this and what I know of long-term weather patterns. I hope to be able to chat with you about this at some point.

Many thanks again for giving me this opportunity.

Yours,

Henry Pukeman

The Master's Lodge,
Sedgwickham,
West Sussex,

11th November, 2009

Re: Youth Business Club

Dear Henry,

I am delighted that you are now going ahead with your plans for this club. I am sure that plenty of our pupils here at St. Cretien's will jump at the chance to learn how to navigate through the perils of our economic maelstrom at the moment, and I don't mind telling you, given last year's financial crisis, and the ongoing troubles on the world markets, that I welcome an activity such as this, which is more necessary than ever.

I would indeed like to talk to you at some point about your theories concerning the application of meteorology to the financial markets, but I have to say I am rather busy at the moment, so it might have to wait for a while. In the meantime, well done, and keep up the good work!

Yours,

A. K. Warble

ALAN WARBLE, BA CANTAB, Dip Ed

ST. CRETIEN'S COLLEGE
WEST SUSSEX

From the Inspection Enforcement Officer

Level: 4A:Inspection (urgent)/5B:Ongoing (urgent)
Marking and Assessment [sec. 4.1 & 4.2]
HBGR-321(a)

Code: «3332-8466»

12th November, 2009

Re: The Inspection, April 19th – 21st, 2010

As you are all aware, the TOFFSTED Inspection is to take place at the beginning of the Summer Term, and I should like to address the issue of marking pupils' work

Over the next few weeks, I shall be taking in exercise books from a sample of each class, from each and every colleague, and I shall hope to see these books marked in a way which conforms to the standards set up at the beginning of the year. If marked work is found to be wanting in any way, the books will be given back to the teacher in question, and s/he will be expected to remark the work, and to add any number of comments deemed appropriate or necessary to bring it up to scratch.

Some examples of comments which we expect to see on marked work are as follows:

> *Stunning presentation, Tracy*/relevant name
> *Excellent arguments, well thought-out, Alfred*/relevant name
> *Impressive exposition of ideas, Nadine*/relevant name
> *Clever use of diacritics, Stanley*/relevant name
> *Brilliant work, Janice*/relevant name, *keep it up!*
> *Superb analysis, Grimeboy*/relevant name, *continue in this vein!*
> *Fine and dandy, Pashtun*/relevant name, *what more can I say? Well done!*
> *See me later, Dravidina*/relevant name

In implementing this directive, please try to avoid using too much paper, if you could.

In extreme cases, where it is felt that the quality of the work/marking done would be detrimental to our passing the Inspection, the decision may be taken to destroy books entirely, and to sit the pupil down over one weekend, in order to copy out her/his work afresh.

Please feel free to speak to me, if you have any queries about this new policy.

Yours in appreciation,

Thomas Horngold

THE CHAPLAINCY
St. Cretien's College

To all House Masters,

Unfortunately, I have need once again of asking you all to be more watchful in Chapel. This week's service was attended by some really appalling behaviour amongst the children, which not only outraged me, making me truly think vengeful thoughts, but left me also devastatingly embarrassed in front of this week's visiting preacher, the Abbot Jeremy Jukes from Jadlington-on-the-Joyle.

What also filled me with peculiar loathing for our pupils was their all-too-successful attempts at instigating Mexican waves each time they were asked to stand or sit, as well as their cheery swaying to the Hymn "Living Lord." It really must be stressed to them to take Chapel more seriously than they do at present, lest they find themselves on the wrong side of my wrath.

In the short term, if things do not improve during services, I will begin a series of House-by-House penitentiary services, each lasting 2½ hours, on Saturday evenings beginning with Scanker's House, to serve as an example of how seriously I am taking this.

The Senior Chaplain

15 / 11 / 09

DIC : 15.11.09

Let None who Enter this House not find Nothing which pleaseth not Some one nor No-one ·Amen·

St Cretien's School Chapel

The Master's Lodge,
Sedgwickham,
West Sussex,

16th November, 2009

Dear Daffyd,

A number of colleagues and I feel that enough time has passed now for us to address the question of your Peace Cave in the Science Block. Whilst it is widely agreed that it was set up with the very best of intentions, and, as you said to Fiona Mullum's parents, represents a "pocket of human warmth within the steely oppression of St. Cretien's," the Senior Management Team has now concluded that it has perhaps served its purpose of drawing attention to your own concerns since September 11th.

Not only have a number of our islamic pupils begun openly to refer the "cave" as their only non-Christian sanctuary, and calling the Revd. Caustick a dangerous infidel behind his back, but some members of staff are troubled that a few pupils are clandestinely smoking and drinking there, claiming "post-traumatic stress" as their justification, despite the fact that many of them were mere toddlers when the events actually happened. Needless to say, as well as being a clear infringement of school rules, evidence of smoking there, among what is very flammable material, would quite reasonably be picked up very quickly by Brian and Barry on Health and Safety grounds.

Although I applaud the initial impetus of your setting up of the Peace Cave, the fact that Mr. and Mrs. Mullum have now withdrawn both Fiona and Peter from St. Cretien's leaves me no alternative other than to ask you to close it down. Furthermore, the fact that the Daily Mail has recently referred to Osama Bin Laden's being harboured within St. Cretien's is proving simply bad publicity for us, which we can sorely do without!

Thank-you for your understanding, and for all your tireless efforts in the school.

A. K. Warble

ALAN WARBLE, BA CANTAB, Dip Ed

School office memorandum – Common room notice board

<u>Saturday Evening Detentions</u>   <u>21 . 11 . 09</u>

Stella Ziggy	single	Putting a spider in a pupil's Mars bar
Sue Percreeps	single	Screaming like a baby
Priam Hardy	double	Strangling a junior's pet
Geoffrey Salad	single	Behaviour in German
Perry Como (?)	single	Smoking
Alison Bend	double	Serious lack of judgment in boys houses
Emily Rosalyn	single	Having inappropriate pin-ups in room
Seline Finghumpton	single	Chewing in lessons (again)
Eleanor Filler	single	Smoking
David Jones	single	Impersonating a lad insane
David Avanaloff	single	Lying to staff about "missing" preps
Trevor Hui-Yang	double	Missing periods 3 & 4, Friday
Gillian Querty	single	Smoking
Hunky Lowe	double	Breaking glass after asking pupil to be his wife
Oscar Uncthorpe	single	Smoking in someone else's bed
Frederick Sallyhope	single	Over-familiarity with animals on Farm
Ash Estuachès	single	Pretending to be a scary monster to juniors
Vaughan Smiler	double	Over-familiarity with a certain member of staff
Benjamin Stroke	single	Behaviour towards new intake
Sally Drippe	single	Pining too much over inevitable heartbreak
Christopher Robin	double	Claims to being on sponsored absence, Tues.
Theo N. White-Duke	single	Being an outsider and a heathen

All detentions will take place in **TMM's room** (Science 9) from 7.30 pm till 10.00
Entrance to disco thereafter will be left to house parent's discretion, case by case.

Mr. Barry Kuller
Housemaster

WELTING HOUSE

Mr. Barry Kuller

To: PIG
Re: Simon Parcel, Fifth Form

Peregrine,

      I wonder if you could see this boy at some point today concerning his behaviour last night, when in full view of his year group peers, he referred to me as "Barry." This unfortunate incident occurred while he and a number of other boys, who have been fantastic value in the House this term, were in my flat, where I had allowed them to socialise at the end of the evening with a bottle of beer between two.

      Imagine my surprise, when in the middle of what was admittedly becoming increasingly relaxed, juvenile banter, the boy in question cheekily referred to me in the third person. I am afraid I erupted with fury, and they all realised that a line had been crossed. When the boy then added that he was only joking, I am sorry to admit I only just refrained from striking the child. I was particularly galled, since the gathering had been intended as a social event, and was utterly ruined by Simon Parcel's outrageous rudeness. I sent them all to bed immediately.

      All the boys in Welting House are aware of the rules I have here, and know that I insist on their abiding by the House rules, regardless of what they claim goes on in other houses. The boy has forfeited all my goodwill to him at present, and I feel that he should at the very least be sent to the School Marshall to pick litter, as well as having a disciplinary detention and a letter home to emphasise just how rudely some of these boys behave when they board here. Do they see this as a holiday camp, I ask?

      Thank-you for your time and effort. I hope I shall sometime soon be able to look this boy in the face again.

Cheers!

Barry

```
X-ViruChekked: Checked
From: Hip@stcretiens.org.uk
Date: Tue, 1 Dec 2009 19:46:43 EST
Subject: Too good to be true!
To: royandbrenda@yahoo.co.uk
X-Mailer: CompuServ 2001 6.0 for Windeyes UK sub 233309
X-MD-d: royandbrenda@yahoo.co.uk
X-Return-Path: hip@school@stcretiens.org.uk
Reply-To: hip@school@stcretiens.org.uk
```

royandbrenda@yahoo.co.uk

Dear Mum and Dad,

Something rather splendid has happened! Do you remember me mentioning our Second Master's circular given out at the beginning of term about catching smokers? Word is, somehow, this has been carelessly allowed to enter the public domain, and the pupils now have hold of the treasure of information within, which not only includes his fear of us appearing threatening to the kiddies, but also gives details of where to find examples of various smokeable substances in the top drawer of his office. Apparently, the Fourth Form have begun to experiment beyond tobacco now, whilst the entire Sixth Form is stoned from dawn till dusk, so great was his accumulation of confiscated skunk etc. So much for the school's drugs policy… And I hear the Head is livid! Even Felix Rompant, the doyen of all House Masters has been solemnly offered dope, though I dare say he accepted some, just in the hope of remaining their close friend and mentor!

Of course, the Upper Sixth are now whimpering whenever they are bust smoking, and a couple have even made complaints to the Head that they feel desperately overwhelmed and threatened whenever two or more staff catch them, and are now demanding that the school pays for post-trauma counselling. One or two have even started having a stash of something really strong at hand, in order to see the staff trying drugs in front of them, as the instructions were perfectly clear that we needed to check what exactly they were smoking. Some of my colleagues are now certainly beginning to look decidedly shell-shocked after their duty day.

You couldn't make it up if you tried.

Are you still coming down here for the end of term? Can't wait to see you both! Actually, there's someone I'd like you to meet. I won't say much more, but I have been a bit involved with some friends I've made, who work on the local paper, and I have been seeing quite a lot of one of them, who will probably join us for a pub lunch while you're down here. She's called Ellie...

Lots of love,

Henry.

THE ST. CRETIEN'S

DEBATING SOCIETY

Please join us in the Library for this week's debate,
followed by tea, coffee and biscuits

This week's motion:

THIS HOUSE BELIEVES THAT THE WHOLE MIDDLE EAST ACTS LIKE A NAUGHTY CHILD

*

Thursday, 7.30 pm

Please ensure you obtain your Housemaster's / Housemistress'
permission beforehand

THE CHAPLAINCY
St. Cretien's College

To all Staff,

Well, another Christmas is upon us, and I must say how lovely it is to see all the children enjoying the six-week build-up we seem to manage to create here at St. Cretien's. The atmosphere has been positively festive now since the middle of October, and the number of films being shown throughout the school this week has made the whole site feel like Cannes! I even noticed on my travels that the Languages Department has renamed its classrooms: "Screen 1," "Screen 2" etc. How very much in the spirit of our Lord Jesus Christ's birthday!

I have a few things to say about the events being lined up for this final week of the term. Firstly, when it comes to the Nativity, although it is always lovely and inclusive to have our Muslim pupils feeling involved in the whole event (we are a Christian school, after all!), I do think we need to think again about allowing some of the more vocal ones to have any roles of importance. The way young Ibrahim Saleh denounced the Virgin birth last year in front of all our parents was most embarrassing, not least because he made Mary herself burst into tears, and caused a fight on stage. Shouting the words "false prophet" repeatedly at the baby doll in the manger, then throwing it out into the audience was not really very good for the school's image. Let's relegate him this year to being a donkey, and have little Mohammed as the quiet king carrying myrrh.

As for the normal services around this time, I would quite like to cut them down a little. Last year in the final week of term we managed to fit in no fewer than eleven separate carol services, and even I was beginning to tire of singing the same old songs over and over again. This wasn't helped by the way the Third Form delivered their agonising version of *O Come All Ye Faithful* and *Ding-Dong-Merrily-On-High*, nor by the fact that the Concert By Candlelight went on for three-and-three-quarter hours. At times I was beginning to doubt my own faith, I won't hide it from you.

So let's see if we cannot condense it all into just a few events this Christmas. And please let's definitely keep the House Parties, as I do always look forward to going from House to House, sampling the mince-pies and having a little taste of the mulled wine generously offered up – I'm sure every year I never make it to the last House, though I am always informed the next day that I did, and my antics are recounted back to me in all their gory detail!

With Season's Blessings,

The Senior Chaplain

4 / 12 / 09

DIC : 4:12:09

Xmas fun day!! Thursday 10th Dec.

Once again, it's that time of year again and so we'll be holding a special

FESTIVE FUNDAY !!!

for the whole school

10.00   -   parents and pupils arrive

10.30   -   staff fancy-dress parade
(please this year can we keep the theme strictly to Xmas, and let's not be too realistic with our costumes, so the pupils can see who is underneath – let's have no repeat of this year's Hallowe'en event, with sixteen witches deliberately going round scaring the living daylights out of the juniors)

11.00   -   All together in Meaddings Hall for opening Xmas cards and exchanging presents

1.00   -   Xmas lunch provided in the Dining Hall; each House to process separately into the Dining Hall with their House staff, sitting quietly at their places until everybody is seated. No crackers to be pulled, no drinks poured, no talking, until the Head Master is seated at High Table, and has said Grace

2.30   -   Return to Houses for the afternoon, and get ready for House Games (please no inter-House dares this year, given the cost of repairing the Chapel roof last time)

7.30   -   Xmas Disco – all staff present please

4. 12. 09: PIG

FROM THE
HEAD OF MUSIC
St. Cretien's College
TREVOR KING

DATE: 4/12/09   **RE:** The New St. Cretien's School Hymn

To all colleagues

Here, at last, is our new School Hymn, which I am proud to present to you on behalf of the School Chaplain, the Second Master, Mr. Simon D'Essise and myself. It is to replace the old one, which was felt to be somewhat out of tune with St. Cretien's modern dynamic in the 21st Century.

> Across the hills so green and lush,
> O'er spire and tower, tree and bush,
> O'er lake, river, house and palace,
> Even faced with spite and malice,
>
> Faced with hardship, loss and grief,
> We know how life is harsh and brief,
> But in this place we'll find our home,
> Where welcome awaits, wheresoe'er we might roam
>
> Anyone with eyes to see,
> Anyone with arm and leg and knee,
> Anyone with feet and hands,
> Anyone with pores and glands,
>
> Anyone with heart that feels,
> Anyone whose mouth needs meals,
> Who's had a look at our Prospectus,
> Will know with what joy this place injects us!
>
> E'en when described in writers' ink witty,
> And scorned by some unfairly as truly a den of iniquity,
> This hallowed sod shall make your life a better one,
> For you'll always be an Old Cretian.

Trevor King

School office memorandum – Common room notice board

Saturday Evening Detentions   5 . 12 . 09

Neil Grinder	single	Offending members of the art dept.
George Humphrey	single	Smoking
Benjamin Blott	single	Swimming without permission or trunks
Geoffrey Salad	double	Behaviour
Eleanor Filler	single	Smoking
Frederick Sanjit	double	Cycling over Mr. Rompant's sausage dog
Trevor Hui-Yang	double	Missing periods 1,2,3 & 4, Saturday
Oscar Uncthorpe	single	Smoking in French lesson
Frederick Sallyhope	double	Disturbing turn of events on the School Farm
Priam Hardy	single	Behaviour and inappropriate response
Graham Graham	single	Painting 666 on the Chapel doors
Vaughan Smiler	single	Asking a certain member of staff out to dinner
Benjamin Stroke	single	In junior dormitory after lights out
Caroline Furrow	single	High heels in gymnastics
Ferundo Balshack	double	Being found in pub by staff out socially
Randy Oswald	single	Defacing notices from the Head Master
Saul Wobbler	single	Crying in order to get out of P.E.
Sion Fantasma	single	Offering her body to the Fifth Form
Pridella Dunker	double	Eating in the toilets to avoid canteen food
Tyrone Byron	single	Urinating in the Head Master's garden at 1am
Sally Delver	single	Starting a petition to replace her House Mistress
Bella O'Nyons	single	Attacking people with medicine balls

All detentions will take place in **TMM's room** (Science 9) from 7.30 pm till 10.00
Entrance to disco thereafter will be left to House Parent's discretion, case by case.

SATURDAY EVENING
STAFF DUTY PATROL REPORT

Date: 5/12/09
Duty Team Leader: Reginald Pompomery
Duty Team: STD, SAG

Fine. No Problems.

RHP

Thank-you Reginald for your concise notes. I am sure you did not get to hear of the bonfires on the rugby pitches, or notice the six fire engines that had to be called out, but I am glad that everything around the centre of the school was nice and quiet for you and your team on Saturday.

Peregrine

ST. CRETIEN'S COLLEGE
WEST SUSSEX

From the Inspection Enforcement Officer

Level: 4A:Inspection (urgent)/5B:Ongoing (urgent)
Roll Calls and Registration [sec. 2.5 & 2.7]
HBGR-666(a)

Code: «3567-9505»

7th December, 2009

Re: The Inspection, April 19th – 21st, 2010

As you are all aware, the TOFFSTED Inspection is to take place between the 19th and 21st of April of next year. There is still a great deal of aspects of school life which will need to be addressed by then, and I trust I can depend on your support for the following initiative unanimously agreed upon by the Council yesterday evening.

From the beginning of next term, there will be a new regime of Roll Calls, sequenced at precisely the points of the school day when their effects will be maximised to full effect. From January, therefore, please could all House Parents and House Tutors on duty adhere to the following times:

6.50	Pre-breakfast House Meeting – whole House
8.00	Post-breakfast Roll Call – Juniors only
8.20	Post-breakfast Roll Call – Seniors only
11.10	Breaktime Audit – whole House, drop-in only
11.25	End-of-Break Audit – whole House; check they have books
1.35	Lunch Roll Call, in Dining Hall – Juniors only
2.00	Lunch Roll Call, in Dining Hall – Seniors only
4.50	Post-lessons Pop-in – whole House
6.35	Dinner Roll Call, in Dining Hall – Juniors only
6.50	Dinner Roll Call, in Dining Hall – Seniors only
7.00	House Evening Roll Call
8.00	Junior Bedtime Roll Call
9.30	Middle School Bedtime Roll Call
10.00	Sixth Form End-of-day Roll Call
11.00	Final check of rooms
11.10	Duty Staff Roll Call by House Parent

In implementing this directive, please try to avoid using too much paper, if you could. Please feel free to speak to me, if you have any queries about this new policy.

Yours in appreciation,

Thomas Horngold

The Master's Lodge,
Sedgwickham,
West Sussex,

9th December, 2009

The Cremblings,
Sydon Whitton Lane,
Little Gedding,
Surrey.

Dear Mrs. Drew,

Thank-you very much for your kind letter of the 6th December, which so clearly outlined some of your concerns regarding Christmas here at St. Cretien's. I have taken the time to look into a number of the issues you raise, and hope to reassure you with some pertinent responses.

First and foremost, it is with sadness that I accept your condemnation of our Santa Claus grotto. Let me assure you, however, that no matter how upset your son Toby was, when confronted with a much-loved figure spluttering and coughing in the manner you so well describe, it was merely our very own Mr. Simon D'Essise who was under all that makeup, and he had no intention of alarming so many of our pupils who went in to visit him.

Suffice it to say that Simon had a particularly bad cold on that day, but he was determined to see the whole event through (in fact, I admit I also put some little pressure on him, since he very often gets out of various school events), and by the time he was sitting in the rather draughty grotto we'd set up for him, he was on all manner of drugs, and not in the best of moods, to say the least. However, in no way does that excuse the kind of language he employed, though in his defence, we did have informal complaints from only fifty-five of the 279 pupils who went in to have a chat with him.

I understand, too, your concerns about the Christmas card extravaganza which takes place from 11am till 1pm. Usually, this is ample time for the children to sit in their groups and with their Houses, a time for socialising, and, of course, for them to open the cards that have been sent to them by their fellow pupils and teachers. I am very sorry that your Toby did not receive any cards this year, and I am sure that it was especially painful given the fact that he himself gave out 792 cards to others. I am sorry he did not even receive any from some of his favourite teachers, despite the hampers you generously passed their way; I can only say I am sorry for the cost you have incurred (which I'm afraid will not be reimbursed in any way, as you request in your letter), and in future I will ensure that there is a minimum pupil number of cards to be received by each pupil.

Finally, to address your complaint that the Christmas Lunch held in the Dining Hall was exactly the same as every school lunch, except for the cutlery having been specially cleaned and polished, this is in fact unfair in the extreme. I can vouch now that the Catering staff spend an inordinate amount of time planning and preparing our festive meals, and I was in talks with them from mid-October about what to do for the Christmas lunch. The fact is, we all decided that lasagna and chips, with baked-beans for vegetarians was what we wanted this year, and I have to say it was delicious to boot! I hope you understand that our Caterers are constantly under great pressure to provide a varied but wholesome menu throughout the school year and for numerous events, and they have my full backing in what they bring to the table!

I do hope this letter addresses your concerns fully, and I look forward to hearing any further opinions you might have through my Second Master, Mr. Peregrine Grueson.

Yours sincerely,

A. K. Warble

ALAN WARBLE, BA CANTAB, Dip Ed

MEMORANDUM from the Second Master

DATE: 9 :12 :09   **RE:** HM Speech

Please note that it is expected that the Headmaster's End of Term Speech on Friday morning should be attended by all teaching staff. Week after week, on Fridays, only a few of the staff have been sitting on the stage with him, and last Friday there were only two of us (thanks TMM). This hardly encourages our pupils to be present. I hope to see a full turn out on Friday, regardless of how much staff decided to celebrate the end of term within the context of the Xmas Funday disco the night before.

9. 12. 09: PIG

Head Master's Speech Notes – End of Michaelmas 2009

(wait for silence) Ex day-o gloria jew ventiss ett sap-yentis... pause... From the Lord cometh the glory of youth and of learning. Please be seated.

wait for settling down...

Well done all of you! You have put behind you another term here at St. Cretien's, and a very successful one at that! allow for murmuring...

I should like to begin by congratulating all those who took part in the excellent performance last night of Harold Pinter's The Caretaker, and a special thank-you to Mr. Pounde, who not only managed to bring in all 149 of the juniors into a play with only 3 characters, but also masterfully achieved a great many of those Pinteresque pauses for which that playwright is so well known. Very well done, all of you! start the applauding - pause for applause.

This term has also seen an excellent result for our debating society, with Peter Victor and Philip Cropper winning through to the final against Bores College, though Dr. Pampo tells me it was a pity they were not quite convincing enough in their argument that Violence Gets You Nowhere! ignore any sniggers... But they still deserve a round of applause anyway. allow for applause

I hear encouraging news from our games masters that the under 14s rugby are making progress, but mustn't lose hope. pause – you know, a victory is not always winning something, as you will find out later in life. And St. Cretien's is a perfect place to learn just such a lesson- dramatic pause – sweep gaze across hall – all of us here at St. Cretien's know full well how to prepare your young minds for failure, and I cannot emphasise enough how dearly we hold that task.

Long pause. straighten up – finger point

Well, let us go home with that thought in our minds; none of us can know what the future holds for us. Some of you will be great successes, some of you less so, some of you may even fall right through society in its – finger quotations for emphasis – conventional sense, but none of you will be failures in an unconventional sense, even if you do not *not* fail unconventionally. And remember, St. Cretien's will have got you there!

Enjoy your Christmas, all of you, even those of you whose religions are not quite the same as all the rest of us here. I wish you a pleasant, relaxing and reinvigorating holiday, and look forward to seeing you all back here in January.

allow for applause to die away

Loud-artay educat-see-onem in nomminy domminy
Praise the Lord in the name of learning.

Left side first please, in an orderly fashion. Follow the monitors, thank-you

HM

Hawthorn Towers,
The Wold

Xmas 2009.

Dear Mr. & Mrs. Farrow,

A small token of our esteem and thanks for all your help with our sons, and especially with keeping Priam in the school - After all we couldn't bear keeping him here with us!!

All the best for the festive period!

The Hardys

LENT TERM

January, 2010

Hello there! Thanks for your support, we all really appreciated the thought, but sadly the Interflora delivery lady has now also been taken captive. The sorry news of young Will's demise has been softened by the announcement of a new baby for Frank Rachett and Shelly Fudge. We are all delighted here and our kidnappers even organised a little do for us, with spicy nibbles, vol-au-vents and other luxuries we're not that used to here; a really touching gesture, we felt. By the way, could someone check if Sheeba, my brown tabby, is still in my flat; she may need feeding. Thanks! **Tim**

The Common Room,
St. Cretien's Coll.,
Sedgwickham,
West Sussex,
Inglaterra.

Dec 01   Camp McGregor
Sir, Another excellent show by our lads on CCF here in the Highlands. The weather has been pretty atrocious, but they all behaved like real soldiers. I am convinced there is some real army material amongst some of these juniors, and this is borne out by the fact that not one of them seems on the surface to show any signs of homosexuality or otherwise! Hope one day you'll keep your word and join us in one of these camps, but in the meantime you'll just keep on getting these postcards during the school holidays. Enjoy yours! See you in Jan! **Tony**

The Head Master,
St. Cretien's College,
Sedgwickham,
West Sussex,
England.

ST. CRETIEN'S LIBRARY

FROM Mrs. HAGGERS
THE LIBRARIAN

02. 01. 10

Welcome back to the new term! Unfortunately, I must report my displeasure at having to chase up the following books borrowed by Common Room. Please ensure that these books are returned as soon as possible! Thank-you.

Geoffrey Bernay	*The Nude in Photos*
Anthony Ingham	*From Drags to Riches -* *Autobiography of Danny La Rue*
Ralph Selton	*Rock Hudson - A life in pictures*
Peregrine Grueson	*Modern Number Theory* *Teaching Algebra* *Templates for Relationships*
Henry Pukeman	*War and Peace* *Sense and Sensibility* *Pride and Prejudice*
Richard Pounde	*The Occult* *Tarot and Palmistry* *Mysticism and Education*
Sandra Grate	*Women in Politics* *Feminist Art*
Raoul Heffer	*Tin-Tin in Tibet* *Asterix and Cleopatra*
Barry Kuller	*Mein Kampf*
Steven D'Essise	*Embroidery and Cross-Stitching*
Tony Adonals	*Guns and Small Arms*

GBH Jan 10

DATES AND TIMES FOR THE START OF
LENT TERM 2010

<u>Monday, January 4th</u>

9.30am	Staff Meeting in Common Room.
11.00am	Common Room Meeting in Common Room.
11.30am	Coffee Break.
12.00 noon	Short talk by Mrs. Hilary Pounde
	Subject: *Marriage Growls: Juggling your life when your husband is a full-time member of a boarding school*
1.00pm	Lunch in the Dining Hall.
2.00pm	INSET Training: *Learning to live with mistakes; raising grades from E to D.* Presentation by Mr. George Perry of St Dunstan's College, Crawley.
5.00pm	Pupils begin arriving back for the start of term.
6.00pm	Dinner.
8.00pm	Roll Call in Boarding Houses.
10.30pm	Lock-up time.

<u>Tuesday, 5th January</u>

8.30am	Chapel for whole School.
9.30am	Lessons begin as per normal day.

01/01/10:PIG

<u>AGENDA FOR STAFF MEETING</u>

Monday, 4th January, 2010

1.   Head Master's business, as follows:
   - Talk on improvement of standards and work ethos amongst staff
   - New strategy on tucking in shirts - *War on Scruffiness!*
   - Update of work in progress on Head Master's Lodge
   - Latest news on Timothy Rent, and plans to set up a petition to send to the Colombian Ambassador

2.   Bursar's business, as follows:
   - Fund-raising events for Lent Term
   - Cutbacks: all lightbulbs in the school to be replaced by 40 Watt bulbs in an effort to save energy
   - Closing windows; all windows will now be shut permanently in order to prevent needless loss of heat in Winter
   - How teaching staff can improve the financial situation through common sense methods and more thoughtful approach to otherwise obviously bad habits
   - Unfortunate and unnecessary expenses incurred during staff Christmas outing to Calais
   - Fears concerning recent attempts to hack into the school's accounting files
   - Regrets concerning the fall-out from the Christmas deal with *Swing Now!*

3.   Second Master's business:
   - Further need to insist on uniform being worn correctly - emphasis on the new campaign *War on Scruffiness!*
   - Staff smoking patrols - plans to implement a new, more child-centred system based on pupil participation and anonymous tipping-off
   - The next fire-practice is to take place on next Friday evening at 11.45; all resident staff are expected to be present and to help

4.   Chaplain's business

5.   Senior Master's business

5.   Director of Studies

01/01/10:PIG

COMMON ROOM MINUTES for January, 2010

Taken by B. O. Kuller

The meeting began good-naturedly with a welcome to Mr. Darren Tolly (DT) and Miss. Stephanie Rental (SR), who have joined us from Johannesburg as this year's GAP students.

Then matters moved immediately to the fiasco surrounding the use of the school for the *Swing Now!* event over Christmas. EFF asked how the school could possibly have been persuaded to involve itself in such an inappropriate venture, but PIG insisted that both the governing body and the Senior Management Team had been approached by the company, and at no time did anyone suspect that they were organising anything other than a Big Band gala evening for what we knew to be customers paying handsome sums of money. RHP asked whether the school ever looked beyond the acquisition of quick cash, but ASI agreed with PIG that at every stage it had seemed perfectly innocent. The fact that what seemed to be a television crew turned up in the afternoon before the event had merely added to a sense that St. Cretien's was "on the up", as the Head had put it.

"On its uppers" suggested TGA much to nobody's amusement, and then TMM added that somebody must have noticed that the nature of the costumes being taken in were distinctly S & M, rather than M & S. Then TIT said he had not fully understood what "swingers" were, and was enlightened by the ever-helpful Power couple sitting either side of him... Mr. Power himself said he and his wife had inadvertently slipped into the event themselves just before PIG and AKW arrived to register their disapproval of that sort of activity, and his wife then protested that she was outraged that the school could ever have allowed such a pornographic event as a fly-on-the-wall documentary about south coast swingers not only to be set up, but then to let it continue. CIH added that her ten-year old son had been the one to discover the event getting into full swing, and he had not spoken to a soul since.

The matter remained unresolved, but PIG gave his assurance that there would be a full inquiry into the matter as soon as the term was under way. He finished by saying that the income generated by letting out the venue to *Swing Now!* might go some way mitigating some of the understandable anger felt by Common Room.

PIG then reminded everyone that the CR's help in smoking patrols would, as ever, be very appreciated; he asked if there would be anyone willing to help him on the first weekend slot this coming Saturday night from 11:30 to 7:30 am. TMM kindly volunteered.

The Director of Studies ASI flagged up a few changes to the calendar; Founder's Day will now consist of lessons 4 and 7, not 3 and 5 as advertised, both of which will now consist of 45 minutes, with a five-minute changeover time, after which there will be an early break, followed by Head Master's assembly. Furthermore the outgoing leg of the French Exchange will now be leaving earlier than advertised, at 10.00.

The newspaper auction was then begun.

- Minutes witnessed and signed off: BOK & PIG

Head Master's Speech Notes – Start of Lent 2010

(wait for silence) Ex day-o gloria jew ventiss ett sap-yentis... pause... From the Lord cometh the glory of youth and of learning. Please be seated.

wait for them to settle down...

Welcome back to St. Cretien's. I hope you had a good holiday, and that you are all refreshed and ready to strike out into new territories during the course of this new term...

wait for applause

A number of trips occurred over the holidays, and I would like to thank Mr. Adonals as ever for taking a group of CCF boys and girls to army camp in Scotland. The Mountain Rescue service were very understanding about what happened, and they understand the school's point of view that it is always important to push young people like yourselves to your limits; St. Cretien's would not be doing its job if everybody were to come back from such ventures totally the same as they left, and bearing that in mind, we will be holding a fund-raising event later in the term for Jeremy Plight and Stephen Fowler, silly bloody buggers.

Long pause. allow for gravitas of moment

On a more serious note, the school has a number of issues to deal with as a community, and one of those is ensuring that, while each and every one of you has an individual identity, of which I am sure you are justly proud, it remains true that the school is first and foremost – pause, finger – a community. Therefore, we cannot accept certain traits which were developing at the end of last term.

Boys, if you will have long hair, please tie it back like the girls. And mindful of the need for sexual equality here, we do not allow the growth of beards among seniors; not only does it look scruffy, but the girls feel unfairly left out!!

allow laughter to die away...

Certain things are not allowed on site. This includes pets, which can cause difficulties for our cleaners. Whilst one may feel some pity for some of the hardships endured by our animals on the school farm, it was unquestionably an error of judgment on one pupil's part to shelter Ollie the school pig last term. Such a lack of common sense resulted in a great deal of mess in the TV room of Cocker's House, and the unnecessary loss of a perfectly happy animal, after his escape.

That is all, ladies and gentlemen. Please get off to lessons, and begin the term well.

Loud-artay educat-see-onem in nomminy domminy
Praise the Lord in the name of learning.

Middle aisle first please, in an orderly fashion. Follow the monitors, thank-you

HM

THE ST. CRETIEN'S

DEBATING SOCIETY

Please join us in the Library for this week's debate,
followed by tea, coffee and biscuits

This week's motion:

THIS HOUSE BELIEVES THAT GEORGE BUSH WAS A MODERN JULIUS CAESAR

*

Thursday, 7.30 pm

Please ensure you obtain your Housemaster's / Housemistress'
permission beforehand

"A UNIQUE OPPORTUNITY" FOR ALL
AGES!!!

Fräulein MANGLE IS RUNNING AN INFORMAL

dissection   WORKSHOP

ALL WELCOME, ROOM 13
THURSDAY 4.00

BIOLOGY DEPRTMT.,
SC.BUILDG

no specialist equipment
needed. just young, healthy
bodies!

snm

St. Crefien's Sports Pavilion
and rugby fields

JOINT INTER-SPORT EXECUTIVE RELEASE

The following list outlines the various responsibilities of the sports staff, including outside coaches and trainers.

Head of Rugby	Mr. Ronald Savage	RBS
Assistant Rugby Coaches	Mr. Trevor Purr	TYP
	Frl. Sonja Mangle	SMM
	Mr. Hugh Gregory	HUG
Head of Football	Mr. Selwyn Almari	SRA
Assistant Rugby Coaches	Mr. Trevor Purr	TYP
	Dr. Michael Storr	MAS
	Mr. Ronald Savage	RBS
Head of Squash	Mr. Daffyd Fang	DAF
Assistant Squash Coaches	Mr. Simon D'Essise	STD
	Mr. Ronald Savage	RBS
	Mrs. Fiona Derry	FAD
Head of Hockey	Mrs. Fiona Derry	FAD
Assistant Hockey Coaches	Frl. Sonja Mangle	SMM
	Mrs. Deborah Jacks	DDJ
	Miss. Rhiannon Ninn	RUN
Head of Netball	Mrs. Deborah Jacks	DDJ
Assistant Netball Coaches	Miss. Rhiannon Ninn	RUN
	Mrs. Fiona Derry	FAD
Athletics Co-ordinator	Mr. Trevor Purr	TYP
Assistants to the A.C.	Mr. Ronald Savage	RBS
	Miss. Rhiannon Ninn	RUN
	Mrs. Marjorie Gagg	MUG
Head of Scaggle	Mr. Simon D'Essise	STD
Assistants to Scaggle	Mrs. Deborah Jacks	DDJ
	Mr. Ronald Savage	RBS
	Miss. Rhiannon Ninn	RUN
Other Sports Coaches	Mr. Ronald Savage	RBS

```
X-ViruChekked: Checked
From: Hip@stcretiens.org.uk
Date: Tue, 06 Jan 2010 16:54:22 EST
Subject: Next weekend!
To: elliehopes@s-herald.org.uk
X-Mailer: CompuServ 2001 6.0 for Windeyes UK sub 233309
X-MD-d: elliehopes@s-herald.org.uk
X-Return-Path: hip@school@stcretiens.org.uk
Reply-To: hip@school@stcretiens.org.uk
```

elliehopes@s-herald.org.uk

Dear Ellie,

Wondered if we could get together again next weekend. I am free from this
Friday afternoon, as there is a special something-or-other feast day,
which means that the whole school takes the morning lessons off, has a
big assembly in the main hall, and then the weekend begins at lunchtime!
I think a few of us are going straight off to the Hare and Hounds, to
celebrate in appropriate style, and a couple of colleagues have said
they're planning to stay there the whole weekend, at least till Sunday
evening, when they've got to be back in the school for Parents'
evening... Apparently that's the only way some of them get through the
event each year!

How would you like to meet up, then, and afterwards go off and do
something nice? There is an exhibition of hinges in Sandworth, I hear, so
I might well drag you along to that, if you're willing...

Hope to hear from you soon (and thinking about you all the time!),

Henry

P255677:wrm2

05/01/10

45a\ref.102
CRNB

ST. CRETIEN'S COLLEGE
WORKS AND MAINTENANCE DEPT.

Re: H&S Directive 41798:5 (e) – Health and Safety Working Committee (HSWC)

Advance notice is hereby given regarding the implementation of H&S Directive 41798:5 (e) in accordance with EU Regulations 335 & 762 of 1996 Commission Report and File 56, pertaining to risks from open fires on site.

It has been brought to the attention of the HSWC that a number of staff houses and flats still have open fires in one or more rooms. There has been a great deal of discussion and debate about this, with relation to the potential risks of an outbreak, and the decision was arrived at whereby we now request that these fires not be used on Health and Safety grounds. This applies especially to those members of staff who are accommodated in a flat within a Boarding House, as any outbreak of fire in such buildings as these, where roof timbers have not yet been replaced by the fireproof plastic girders, would quickly lead to a major conflagration, with the threat of many unnecessary injuries and fatalities.

We understand that these "period-style" fires have some romantic glamour attached to them, and are in many ways more effective than the heating systems the school installed in the mid eighties. In fact, we at the HSWC would be the first to admit what a shame it would be not to use them. However, we are sure you understand how paramount it is to ensure St. Cretien's remains first and foremost a safe environment for the members of the community who live and work here.

The Lyme & Co. cement works have pencilled next Thursday (17th January) to come round the site and block up all our flues.

Thank-you for your comprehension.

Brian Blouse, GWTO, c/o HSWC

BB : GWTO : 05/01/10

NEW TO ST.CRETIEN'S COLLEGE!

ARE YOU INTERESTED IN **MONEY**?
WANT TO LEARN MORE ABOUT WHAT MAKES

THE WORLD GOES ROUND?

FANCY YOURSELF AS A BIT OF A

WHEELER DEALER?

COME TO THE FIRST MEETING OF THE

YOUTH
ENTERPRISE
CLUB

Every Friday lunchtime in Mr. Pukeman's class

Memo: From MAS

DATE: 08/1/10   **RE:** Sonja's Afternoon Clubs

Peregrine,
          I am writing confidentially in order to express my deep concern with regard to Sonja Mangle's regular workshops; can I be the only member of staff who baulks at the goings-on in New Science Block Room 13 every Thursday afternoon?

Who has done any viable risk-assessment for the industrial heavy-welding equipment she gets the pupils (some as young as 13) to use? Or the smelting processes she employs? Who would be responsible for any injuries sustained in her knife-throwing classes? And who in their right mind could even begin to contemplate the idea of allowing teenagers to handle circular saws, as happened recently when a traumatised tutee of mine went along to a human dissection workshop?

If people are not aware of what is going on, then I feel very strongly that we should be preparing for some lawsuits flying our way pretty soon, something I am sure you agree we can ill afford at the moment.

Yours,

Michael Storr

MAS: 8.1.10

FROM
ST. CRETIEN'S COLLEGE
SECURITY

NO PARKING

This vehicle is parked in contravention of
almost every conceivable directive ever published
by the St. Cretien's Security Department. If it ever
appears here again we shall be obliged to
take the matter further, and destroy it

Thank-you and enjoy your stay in St. Cretien's!

ST. CRETIEN'S COLLEGE
WEST SUSSEX

From the Inspection Enforcement Officer

Level: 4A:Inspection (urgent)/5B:Ongoing (urgent)
Teaching Environment [sec. 6.1 & 6.2]
HBGR-677(a)

Code: «2789-5774»

9th January, 2010

Re: The Inspection, April 19th – 21st, 2010

As you are all not doubt aware, the TOFFSTED Inspection is to take place this very year. And as the big moment gets closer, it is time to address the thorny issue of our teaching environment.

I spent a good number of days over the Christmas holidays wandering around the school, and especially into the classrooms. I must say, I was quite appalled by what I saw. Not only were a number of rooms simply dirty and untidy, but many had hardly any displays on the walls, and in those that did, all I found were half-hearted efforts, with black-and-white photocopies, where there should be bright, colourful posters, alongside pupils' own work. Unbelievably, one teacher has basically photocopied all the textbooks he uses, and stuck these up on the walls, whilst another colleague has endless lists of pupils' names, recording who has or has not got their homework done on time. This is all well below-par.

Most striking of all was a whole department, that clearly thought it acceptable to allow the newly-painted classroom walls to have pupils' graffiti all over them, some of which was of a disgusting nature. I am amazed that they could consider this an appropriate environment for the education of our pupils, not least as much of the more offensive graffiti was directed against the subject taught in those very classrooms. On top of this, most of it was badly spelled, which our inspectors are bound to pick up on.

Therefore we are going to have a school-wide *Tidy Evening* in which all staff and pupils on detention will retire into all the classrooms and sort this situation out once and for all. *Tidy Evening* will take place next Tuesday, from 6.30 until it is done to the satisfaction of the SMT, who will all be walking around informally, making sure that our orders are being carried out. Paint will be provided where necessary (magnolia emulsion).

Please feel free to speak to me, if you have any queries about this new policy.

Yours in appreciation,

Thomas Horngold

School office memorandum – Common room notice board

Saturday Evening Detentions   09 . 1 . 10

Priam Hardy	single	Cannabis racket
Gillian Querty	single	Smoking
George Humphrey	single	Smoking
Ngana Bellamy	single	Smoking
Arthur Primrose	single	Howling during prep time
Dora Grimey	single	Being difficult
Olivia Grunter	single	formulating rude names for members of staff
Perry Como (?)	single	Behaviour
Trevor Hui-Yang	single	Missing period 1, Wednesday
Oscar Uncthorpe	double	Drinking and smoking in bed
Eleanor Filler	single	Smoking
Frederick Sallyhope	double	Unsavoury events on the School Farm
Graham Graham	single	Daubing goat's blood on the Chaplain's door
Vaughan Smiler	double	Abusive behaviour towards a member of staff
Benjamin Stroke	single	Spying on juniors
Simon Cnut	double	Aggression towards innocent cleaners
Christopher Robin	double	Fake claims of being sponsored by Adidas to wear their trainers
Alison Frunke	double	Removing windscreen wipers from staff cars
Ginger Mungo-Rowan	single	Telling visitors how he hated the school
Sally Delver	single	Being found in a boy's room Weds. morning

All detentions will take place in **TMM's room** (Science 9) from 7.30 pm till 10.00
Entrance to disco thereafter will be left to House Parent's discretion, case by case.

SATURDAY EVENING
STAFF DUTY PATROL REPORT

Date: *9/1/10*

Duty Team Leader: *Trevor King*

Duty Team: *RP, FAD*

Not a bad evening at all. I let the other two in my team (Roger Pampo and Fiona Derry) do the initial scout around, before it became too busy, while I was able to fortify myself for the serious work once the disco got underway. I coordinated my duty from the staff bar, and was able to watch for any trouble from the top window, at first, until I found myself too tired to negotiate the stairs up to it, whereupon I was able to call on the other two (Roger Pampo and Fiona Derry) to go out and about to check on the disco. They assured me there was nothing particular going on, so we shared a toast to another quiet, successful Saturday night at St. Cretien's, thanks to the firm hand the top management keep to maintain the iron discipline of these pupils here.

I am closing off now, and have nothing more to say, except that I am going to stay here now, where it's warm. Goodnight, god bless! I really love you all!

THK

Oh dear, oh dear! You must have somehow missed the events down in the School Farm, where some of our more annoying pupils freed the llama, and let him rage all over the site. The disco people are claiming quite a substantial sum indeed for the equipment that was damaged.

Never mind, thank-you all for your hard work this weekend, and yes, Trevor, I think we at St. Cretien's can be proud of the way in which we keep such tight control over 550 pupils without any major incidents each weekend.

Peregrine

Lycée Galtière,
Rue S. Sébastien,
Thillery-la-Crécie,
Pas de Calais

The 12 january, 2010

To the Head of French,
St. Cretiens College,
West Sussex,
UK.

Dear Reginald,

Thank you very much for your detailings concerning the coming-up exchange between our two schools in this coming April. I have enclosed ours lists for the thirty-two pupils at this end of the line, but there are still few points to be added with for.

To begin, an outline of the program we will be laying for your pupils to be getting on with doing. As you are thereof already aware, there is a great deal to be exploring in Thillery-la-Crécie especially at that time in the year, when we will be holding the Festival of the Waters, celebrating our former status as a heath-spa; clearly this eventment will provide an occasion for all our studiants to be spending the day together at this. We have also organised a visit to the local leisure center, and a tour of the generators under it, where of up about to 40% of the towns' waters is recycled and heated; this is always a populare visiting-attraction for the guests at our region.

There will also be taking place a trip to the famous French themes park *Cheeseland*, where visitors are being able to sample various types and distinct varieties of regional, national, and international cheeses. I would have had hoped that we could possibly might be being able to be doing visiting this on the Tuesday, as I had had to have had booked for Monday our fulmost tour of the outlying factory of lubrication, as they're are only accepting tours on the said day. Finally, the visite to the brewery locale is booked for the Thursday, where one is going to be being able to display to us the workings of this former award-winning place of beermaking production. There will be a disgusting period afterward for the visitors to be in a position to sample this fine and typical french product that is now made in Shang-hai.

Concerning the list of pupils, I ought to mention to you that I do notice a number of potential areas of problematical difficulties; Jean-Jacques Choqueur will be needing especial care regarding the family wherein he will be placed, given his history of violence (as attached). Daniel Farouq eats nothing but pork, as a protest against his muselin parents, and finally, Ines insists that she stays with an older pupil, as she is now 19½ years old, smokes the pott, has a little daughter-child at home, and has re-sat her last few years.

Please write me soon if there is any problems regarding this program, but for the meantime, à bientôt!

Agnès Lamartine

P255677:wrm2

13/01/10

45a\ref.102
CRNB

ST. CRETIEN'S COLLEGE
WORKS AND MAINTENANCE DEPT.

<u>Re: H&S Directive 41809:2 (d) – Health and Safety Working Committee (HSWC)</u>

Advance notice is hereby given regarding the implementation of H&S Directive 41809:2 (d) in accordance with EU Regulations 335 & 762 of 1996 Commission Report and File 56, pertaining to risks from open fires on site.

It came to Brian's attention this week that there remains in the Common Room a large open fire of the sort mentioned in our statement last week in the H&S Directive 41798:5 (e). Not only is this in a most sensitive area of the school, being situated in the heart of a building roofed with wooden rafters, but the room itself is wood-panelled, and filled with furniture which does not even begin to comply with EU fire regulations.

On top of this, an incident occurred during the school day on Monday last, which underlines how dangerous such a large fireplace can be without adequate supervision. Brian has learned from a reliable source that when the fire is lit, piled high with flammable kindling wood and the like, such an initial updraught is triggered off so as to constitute a real and imminent threat to life. TIT who stood nearby was literally swept off his feet, and was only able to save himself from being sucked up by deftly clinging on to the fire guard (which, thankfully was not too hot to the touch, since the fire had not been lit until then – but, another potential hazard...).

It might also explain why the Common Room has had four butlers in the past one-and-a-half years, each of whom has disappeared without trace. Brian is now looking into this matter separately. In the meantime, we hope you will understand why we have asked the Lyme & Co. cement works to do the same to the Common Room flue as the other offending flues.

Thank-you for your support in helping St. Cretien's community help itself.

Barry Soddum, GWTO, c/o HSWC

BS : 13/01/10

Hello all! Things are getting a bit hot out here. So far we're all still safe and smiling, but we have had to move again, this time because we seem to have been sold as some kind of slave workforce, making explosives in the most unappetising place imaginable. Pat, our lady from Interflora, has been a real source of inspiration for the pupils, organising small acts of resistance and sabotage, though Terence Wang did follow her advice too far and we all tease him now with the nickname Molotov Cock! Wish you were here, (ho ho!) Love from all the kids to their families back home! Bye!   *Tim*

The Common Room,
St. Cretien's Coll.,
Sedgwickham,
West Sussex,
Inglaterra.

ST. CRETIEN'S COLLEGE
WEST SUSSEX

FROM THE SECOND MASTER

Second Master's Lodge,
15th January, 2010

RE: PRIVATE TUTORIALS

It has been brought to my attention that a number of staff tend to hold tutorials in private even until late into the night, even with alcohol. In order to avoid any unnecessary criticism from the social services, the following guidelines may prove useful.

1. Always ensure that a door giving out onto a public corridor or area is open at all times, and remain close to this open door or sit in a line affording as much visibility as possible. If a tutorial happens to go on longer than approx. 15 minutes, then it might be a good idea to show yourself at the door at regular intervals, and to greet loudly whoever is present, so as to make others aware that you are holding a tutorial.

2. Conduct your tutorial very loudly. This will make your presence clearer to any potential witnesses, and may also make clear to them as to the content of your conversations. This measure need not be limited to just raising your voice, but should also extend to moving furniture around, placing pencils loudly down on tables and walking around heavily.

3. Always place a piece of furniture between yourself and the pupil, or, if there is nothing practical to hand, then place your own chair at an angle, so as not to be facing your pupil directly. Never position your seat directly in front of the pupil's, never invade their space by leaning forward too intimately, and never stand over them while holding your tutorial, as this can be misconstrued now as threatening behaviour.

4. Take detailed minutes. The worth of these in a court of law clearly does not need to be spelled out.

5. Avoid at all times any conversation of a suggestive nature, and make no references to sex or masturbation. The following words should certainly be avoided: piss; shit; w*nk; f*ck/f*cker/f*cking; arse; breasts; c**t; bloody; bleeding; bugger/ buggering/ buggery; hot-pants; kinky; 69er; missionary; doggy, dogging, cottaging, hamfister, fisting, felching, p**ting, or**ging, r****ling, gangm****ling, dr***p**ing, cr**ting, etc.

Thank-you for your understaining.

15/01/10:PIG

School office memorandum – Common room notice board

Saturday Evening Detentions   16 . 1 . 10

Mungo Rant	single	Behaviour in sex education lesson
Eleanor Filler	single	Smoking
Gillian Querty	single	Smoking
George Humphrey	single	Smoking
Priam Hardy	double	Threatening behaviour to Mrs. Greet's newborn
Harry Dercules	single	Being downright clever by half
Sally Delver	single	Inappropriate response to film about Nazis
Billy Bottock	single	Baiting PC Evelyn Hall in town
Trevor Hui-Yang	double	Missing Chapel
Oscar Uncthorpe	single	Drinking in PE lesson
Jennifer Thwaite	single	Smoking
Frederick Sallyhope	single	Misplaced affection for certain animals on farm
Graham Graham	double	Nailing his own 95 theses on Chapel door
Vaughan Smiler	double	Lavishing inappropriate gifts on staff
Benjamin Stroke	single	Taking juniors off for "nature ramble"
Duncan Bludgenstone	double	Teasing girls with a tarantula
Philip Felcher	single	Mocking the entire Arab world in a presentation
Serena Dump	single	Asking her teachers too many personal questions
Nigel Mantap	single	Playing heavy metal music too loudly in room
Quentin Seljuk-Crisp	double	Plagiarising his entire year's work so far
Olivia Viable	single	Never saying "please" and "thank-you"
Sonya Berembular	single	Sighing when being given very useful advice

All detentions will take place in **TMM's room** (Science 9) from 7.30 pm till 10.00
Entrance to disco thereafter will be left to House Parent's discretion, case by case.

ST. CRETIEN'S COLLEGE
WEST SUSSEX

From the Inspection Enforcement Officer

Level: 4A:Inspection (urgent)/5B:Ongoing (urgent)   Code: «2774-4886»
Staff Conduct and Behaviour [sec. 7.1 & 7.2]
HBGR-889(c)   21st January, 2010

Re: The Inspection, April 19th – 21st, 2010

As you all know, there has to be a great deal of serious thought spent on getting our systems and structures in place, especially as we failed our last HMC Inspection, and were closed for a fortnight until we could account for all the missing pupils (Whinny Butt never did turn up, alas).

Bearing this in mind, the SMT Inspection Rapid Reaction Unit has decided to implement a policy of no alcohol on site at all, in the run-up to the Inspection itself, i.e; from the beginning of the Easter Holidays onwards, in order to acclimatise ourselves to this new situation. Of course, staff may quite reasonably continue to enjoy the occasional tipple (and a tipple means just a tipple, for those of you in the Music Dept who do not understand the concept, mentioning no names), but this will, from 2nd April, have to take place off-site. Naturally, this will set an excellent example to our pupils, who over the years have witnessed far too much gritty realism, as far as staff behaviour is concerned when alcohol is involved.

This will also be the case for the few members of staff who still smoke, though the less we dwell on this the better, since it is clear to all other, sane members of staff that this particular rule will be doing you a favour in the long term.

We hope you will feel able to wholeheartedly support us in this initiative, and will give us your full support. Obviously, we don't wish to impinge too heavily on your own, individual lifestyles, but should be noted that we have informed Security of this decision, which will mean that not only will they have the right to ask staff to desist from having alcohol on site, and may even feel the need to conduct random searches of staff flats and houses, but also they too will now not be inebriated whilst on duty.

Please feel free to speak to me or anyone else on my team, if you have any queries about this new policy, or if you wish to take issue with anything in this memo.

Yours in appreciation,

Thomas Horngold

JEH

PLEASE WOULD YOU COVER THE FOLLOWING LESSON FOR: EFF

PERIOD: 3   DAY: Mon   DATE: 1ˢᵗ Feb

MANY THANKS.

Jeremy,

Thanks for covering this 5ᵗʰ Form Class. They are generally OK, but all rather critical. I have left them some work to do on trigonometry from their revision books and they should do as much as they can. If they finish, they can go on to start their prep, which is p 25 in their textbooks, Ex 1, 2, 3, + 4

They will try to tell you that I have never covered this stuff with them, but don't believe a word they say. Whatever you do, DO NOT TEACH THEM. I will never hear the end of it, and they'll expect it every lesson. What's more, they do not deserve it. For now, just tell them you don't understand trigonometry yourself, and use the period for yourself!

Thanks again for covering them,

Eamon

School office memorandum – Common room notice board

Saturday Evening Detentions   6 . 2 . 10

Trevor Hui-Yang	double	Missing periods 3 & 4, Thursday
Priam Hardy	single	Blocking sinks in boys' toilets
Geoffrey Salad	single	Behaviour
Eleanor Filler	single	Smoking
Richard Bamber	single	Drinking
Vincent Wang	single	Drinking
Vaughan Smiler	single	Threatening behaviour
Petula Botuler	single	Drinking
Jennifer Thwaite	single	Climbing pylons
Seline Finghumpton	single	Silly singing in Chapel
Pippa Deller-Jones	single	Lewd behaviour
Oscar Uncthorpe	single	Skinning up in House detention
Frederick Sallyhope	single	Unhealthy interest in Kylie on the School Farm
Benjamin Stroke	single	Smoking (thank-god)
Rhiannon Hacker-Smith	double	Insisting on pink ink in her English tests
Tamsin Silke-Tyrone	single	Shouting over her teacher
Spike Ferret	double	Speaking without thinking
Cedric Funque-Proude	single	Refusing to help clear up his friend's vomit
Siegfried Humboldt	double	Smirking within earshot of teachers' chatting
Dermot Otterbreath	double	Being on the computers at 4am
Kieran McDandifloe	single	Yelling out at the public from a minibus
Bronte Gracchus-Helios	double	Praying in a silly voice

All detentions will take place in **TMM's room** (Science 9) from 7.30 pm till 10.00
Entrance to disco thereafter will be left to House Parent's discretion, case by case.

COMMON ROOM NOTICE BOARD

A number of pupils are insisting they have the right to sit out lessons in protest at the continuing US presence of Afghanistan. I have made the school's position on this perfectly clear, and so that none of our colleagues are confused about this, it is as follows:

No pupil should be exempted from full-time lessons or activities, unless they have a note from their local imam, and this needs to be in English; last week Alquq Aziz convinced a number of teachers that the writing on a fraudulent letter was Arabic, whereas in fact he had simply pilfered some of Raoul Ganger's prep, and we all know how poor *his* handwriting is…

If pupils wish to exercise their right to protest, then they should do so only in their free time, and only by visiting Daffyd Fang's new Afghan Peace Tent, which has now replaced his Peace Cave in the lobby of the Science Block.

Certainly we must avoid the kind of appalling behaviour we saw at the weekend amongst our small but vociferous Islamic pupil body; there is absolutely no place at St. Cretien's for Bible burning, and I feel sure that we are infringing on no-one's Human Rights (as was claimed) if we insist on this.

If there are any more queries, please don't hesitate to chat with me about it.

Anthony Ingham

Anthony Ingham, Director of Studies

St. Cretien's Combined Cadets Forces

Tony G. Adonals

Please note all members of staff and pupils:

Due to recent CCF manoeuvres, the croquet lawn at the Lower Backs is **strictly out of bounds**, having been requisitioned last week for mine-planting practice. With the whereabouts of some of these mines still not in all cases accounted for, over the next few days, I will be putting the boys and girls responsible onto the case of finding them again! In the meantime, I ask you all for your patience.

Thanking one and all!!

Tony

TGA/CCF/HTTH/FO/09.02.10

The Master's Lodge,
Sedgwickham,
West Sussex,

9th February, 2010

Tony,

I am writing with a great deal on my mind about certain tidings I have heard recently regarding your running of the CCF. It has come to my attention that you have all this time been using live ammunition with the pupils, and that on one occasion during the CCF camp at half term, one boy came very close to losing his life. I can only be grateful that we have managed to avoid disaster before now. Furthermore, I discover through a casual message pinned to the CR Notice Board that our Croquet Lawn is presently out of bounds due to its being laced with anti-personnel mines.

I cannot exaggerate enough the dangers in which this policy places our pupils, and I think you will understand my deep concern for all aspects of safety here at St. Cretien's, whether on the site or away with members of staff. I am fully aware of your personal passion for and pride in all matters military, and I know I echo many colleagues' thoughts in saying how much we appreciate your involvement and commitment in this field of the School's life. However, I must now insist that no more live weaponry be used for CCF; I feel I ought to add that the only reason it has continued up till now was due to my and my team's ignorance of the facts.

Please pop in to talk to me further on the matter, but take this letter as written warning of my views on what the School's policy will henceforth be.

A. K. Warble

ALAN WARBLE, BA CANTAB, Dip Ed

The Cremblings,
Sydon Whitton Lane,
Little Gedding,
Surrey.

12th February, 2010

The Head Master,
St. Cretien's College,
Sedgwickham,
West Sussex.

Mr. Warble,

It is with regret that I am writing to you about the injury sustained by my son, Toby, who was involved in an accident this week while on manoeuvres with CCF. Furthermore, it is with shock that I learn that your master in charge of CCF, a certain Mr. Adonals, has been using no less than live bullets each Wednesday afternoon with boys and girls as young as thirteen. I find it at present difficult to express my outrage at the way your school has allowed this to persist for so long, and I hold you personally responsible for Toby's unfortunate mishap.

In this day and age, when schools and colleges are becoming so conscious of the need for due care and safety, I would have expected a modicum of intelligence when dealing with young teenagers handling military hardware. The fact that Toby will now have a permanent, scarred parting across his once-lovely head of hair will serve, I hope, as a stark reminder to yourself and those who work in your establishment of a school's responsibility when it comes to matters of safety.

We are expecting St. Cretien's to compensate us for the cost of the cosmetic surgery Toby will have to undertake, as well as for the stress he has unnecessarily been caused. If negotiations to this end do not meet our satisfaction, then we will certainly be taking our story to the national press.

Yours sincerely,

S.R. Drew (Mrs.)

The Master's Lodge,
Sedgwickham,
West Sussex,

15th February, 2010

The Cremblings,
Sydon Whitton Lane,
Little Gedding,
Surrey.

Dear Mrs. Drew,

Thank-you very much indeed for your letter of the 12th February, outlining your concerns for the way we run our Wednesday afternoon CCF activity. May I take this opportunity immediately to express how much we here at St. Cretien's College appreciate parents' comments on both our strengths and our weaknesses; we are certainly aware of some areas in which we can improve the service we offer, and I personally welcome constructive criticism and open debate.

There are most definitely aspects of the CCF which need swift attention, and a number of these have already been dealt with, such as the use of live ammunition, the exploitation of the juniors as dummies for bayonet-practice and the slightly inconvenient habit of leaving areas of the school mined. However, please rest assured that all of these awkward inconsistencies and more have now been ironed out! At present our Health and Safety Officers are looking at the matter, and drawing up plans to reduce the chances of such injuries happening again.

Of course, I sympathise entirely and genuinely for Toby, and I understand fully the distress he must be suffering. However, I do not hold the school totally responsible for his injury, as the Master in charge of CCF assures me that Toby himself had not been behaving in an appropriate way at the time the rifle exploded, so I regret to inform you that we will not be offering any financial compensation to you or your son. However, in view of your valued custom, as well as your son's contribution to the life of the School, the Governors and I would like to offer him a reduction in the cost of his CCF trip to West Wales, if you still felt it was appropriate for him to go away with Mr. Adonals.

As an aside, I would also ask you not to be too hasty in committing Toby to any permanent cosmetic surgery in the short term, as Mr. Almari, the Head of Drama, has expressed his hope that he might be persuaded, given his unfortunate scar, to play the part of Harry Potter in this summer's Junior Play, based on the film.

I hope you understand and respect our position on this matter, and I hope too that you do not resolve to take your story to the any newspaper. We at St. Cretien's have an excellent record of dealing well with such publicity.

Yours sincerely,

A. K. Warble

ALAN WARBLE, BA CANTAB, Dip Ed

ST. CRETIEN'S COLLEGE
WEST SUSSEX

From the Inspection Enforcement Officer

Level: 4A:Inspection (urgent)/5B:Ongoing (urgent)   Code: «2750-1895»
Personal Behaviour [sec. 8.12 & 8.13]
HBGR-446(d)   13th February, 2012
Re: The Inspection, April 19th – 21st, 2010

As I am sure I don't need to remind you, the Inspection is now looming, and it strikes me that there is still one important area we, as staff, need to address. This is the inevitable question of toilet visits.

I happen to know that a number of staff consider it perfectly normal to leave a lesson mid-way through teaching, with a full class sitting there in front of them, in order to relieve themselves. Now, while some amongst our colleagues might plead old age as your excuse (and I accept there are a select few who may well be justified, though that brings up the whole question of retirement age...), the SMT do feel it is quite inexcusable for this habit to continue. In recent months, there have even been suggestions that staff have been arranging to meet at certain times for a toilet break, in order to have a chat, or even a smoke; at one point last Wednesday, it was reported to me that a total of thirteen male members of staff were heard to be chatting loudly and laughing in the gents' toilets, when all of them should have been in classes. As for Rodney and Olivia Powell, one can't even communicate from the gents' to the ladies' toilets, so god knows where they disappear to.

From now on, it will be stated clearly in the school handbook that staff must do their utmost not to leave their lessons in order to answer nature's calls. This can be facilitated by having only one, small coffee at break-times, drinking less water in general, and making sure that one has already gone to the toilet just before the end of break; on this last point, even if one does not feel the need at the time, I find it often helps just being in the environment, with people around me going, before getting the urge myself, and with only a little straining. As a last resort, small, discreet colostomy bags could be provided, as a failsafe way of being able to stay in the classroom. I have one myself, and I find it is actually quite satisfying to know I am seeing to nature's call while standing there teaching, say, the Third Reich.

One footnote to all this concerns Toby Standard, who has recently got into the habit of being so desperate now, after holding things in for too long, that he instinctively begins to open his flies before getting to his destination; last week, he began the procedure as early as the upstairs corridors, and this is not what we want the Inspectors to see. Please, if you see him like this, tell him to put it away, and don't make a big thing of it.

Thomas Horngold

School office memorandum – Common room notice board

<u>Saturday Evening Detentions</u>   <u>13 . 2 . 10</u>

Timothy D'Alton	single	Threatening to kill another pupil
Graham Graham	single	Replacing Chapel icons with porn
Shaun Konry	single	Scraping off valuable gold leaf with his finger
Frederick Sallyhope	single	Attempting to stage a marriage on farm
George L'Asenbay	double	Telling a visitor he works for the Queen
Benjamin Stroke	single	Cooking nibbles at midnight for juniors
Danny Craigh	double	Organising a right royal betting game
Roger More	double	Having eight girls in his room
Piers Brosinane	single	Claiming he would die the next day
Vaughan Smiler	double	Disappearing inexplicably for too long
Iain Phlegming	single	Telling tall tales
Oscar Uncthorpe	single	Smoking in bus on theatre trip
Gerard Blowfield	single	Scaring the living daylights out of women
David Knivven	single	Being unnecessarily charming to everyone
Trevor Hui-Yang	double	Missing Assembly
Silas Petticoat	single	Recording teachers for offensive ring tone
Jennifer Thwaite	single	Smoking
Seline Finghumpton	single	Chewing in lessons
Priam Hardy	single	Obnoxious presence in Chemistry
Nick Knack	double	Impersonating a dwarf
Skye Foole	single	Claiming to be 23 while in a pub
Liv Anladye	single	Practising voodoo

All detentions will take place in **TMM's room** (Science 9) from 7.30 pm till 10.00
Entrance to disco thereafter will be left to House Parent's discretion, case by case.

SATURDAY EVENING
STAFF DUTY PATROL REPORT

Date: *13/2/10*
Duty Team Leader: *Rodney Power*
Duty Team: *GAS, EJS*

I spent a little while doing patrols, but had to pop back home to help Olivia with the cooking and such like, but when I re-emerged later, my two colleagues in tonight's team had already put a number of the pupils in their places, i.e. back to Houses! Anyway, had to pop back again a while later, as Olivia and I had to meet up at a certain time for personal reasons. By the time I finished duty, it seemed all very quiet to me. Edward and Gwendoline had headed off to the bar, so I returned to Olivia, who needed some attention by then, and bid goodnight to the school for the night. And next morning, if I'm lucky !

RAP

Thanks Rodney. Much appreciated. I dealt with the police detectives myself at half-past midnight, which I really don't mind at all; after all, it's my job !

Peregrine

FROM
ST. CRETIEN'S COLLEGE
SECURITY
PLEASE NOTE!

Over the next two months, the temporary office buildings which presently house the St. Cretien's Security HQ is to be demolished and replaced with a new, upgraded security complex, more suited to the needs of the Defence Unit in a modern school. Although we have managed to continue to provide a basic level of support and security in the present block, it has become hopelessly inadequate, especially as the security remit in recent years has had to expand to include new threats and dangers, including the importation of illegal kebabs and drugs onto the site, the risk from unknown and unidentifiable paedophiles in the area, and of course the constant threat of international terrorism. The new Security HQ will include a state of the art raising barrier, sandbags will be replaced by proper tank-proof banks, and the main bunker, at a total depth of 30 meters will be serviced by over 1½ miles of bomb-proof tunnels. We are all very excited indeed here about the prospect of our move into these much needed facilities, and look forward to putting them to good use in defending our way of life here at St. Cretien's.

MEMORANDUM from the Second Master

DATE: 16:02:10   **RE:** Forged Signature

Could staff please pay particular attention to any memos purporting to be from the Head of Music. Trevor has been very aware recently of a spate of fraudulent letters, signed in his name.

Trevor became alerted to the problem when an unduly large number of colleagues were approaching him about letters excusing pupils from academic lessons, letters with Trevor's signature on, which were thrust under colleagues' noses. Obviously, no-one suspected the truth at the time, though at the point that Timothy Munt realised that there were consistently 22 pupils out of his Third Form Physics class (out of a total of 23), alarm bells did begin to ring with us in the Senior Management Team.

It transpires that one or two pupils managed to copy and perfect Trevor's signature, and started running a small racket selling letters absenting pupils, some of whom didn't even play an instrument. Suspicion really should have been aroused when Benjamin Pott announced that he needed to be excused from Chemistry in order to take his Grade 8 harp exam; this is the boy, after all, who was incapable of singing "We are the Champions" at last summer's Rock Concert, and who couldn't even play the triangle in time, at the Juniors' Summer Musical.

Therefore, in future, after consultation with Trevor, the SMT has decided that he should sign all his official correspondence in his blood. This should immediately make any forgeries stand out, as well as putting the culprits off doing it any more. If they do begin to use blood themselves, then we can perform a DNA test on it, to ascertain its provenance.

Please therefore be aware of any notices/letters/memos from the Head of Music, which are not simply in black and white!

Thank-you for your vigilance.

Peregrine

16. 02. 10: PIG

The St. Cretien's
Christian Union
is meetin' next thurs

7.30pm
in the
Chapel Crypt

Subject: "Why is GOD just so f**king cool?!"

Yo, hang out dudes!!

FROM THE

HOUSE MASTER OF DREER HOUSE

To: Priam Hardy   **Date:** 18th February   **Re:** German lessons

Priam,

    Please drop into my office tonight after 10:30, to discuss over a civilised glass of wine the small matter of a certain type of Hardy-esque behaviour which has reached my ears today.

D. M. F.

DMF:18.2.2010

HOUSE MASTER OF DREER HOUSE

To: PIG   **Date:** 19th February   **Re:** German lessons

Peregrine,
      I had strong words yesterday evening with Priam Hardy, and impressed upon him the gravity of his situation. He regretted deeply his approach to Henry Pukeman's lessons, and particularly his poor performance this week.

He assures me that he will definitely turn over a new leaf as far as his attitude is concerned, and I have to say that frankly he does appear most contrite. Seen from the other side of the fence, however, I must also emphasise how very helpful Priam has been so far this term, and I would also point out that his recent grades suggest his academic work is proving extremely promising for a Lower Sixth scholar.

I have underlined to Priam the importance of treating all his teachers with the same level of respect, regardless of any personal conflict which may develop between a pupil and his teacher, and I trust him to maintain this attitude. I also emphasised how it is to be patient with new teachers, even those who are still finding their feet, and unsure of how to deal with real, classroom situations, and regardless of how good they are at actually teaching.

I now consider the matter to be closed, and hope that Henry Pukeman will at least address a pupil's House Master first, rather than trouble Senior Management with any difficulties he may have in his classes.

D. M. F.

DMF:19.2.2010

Dreer House
19.2.10

Dear Mr. Pokeman,

I am really very sorry for my behavour this week in your lessons, and I would like to take this opportunity to assure you it won't happen again. I have spoken with my housemaster Mister Farrow, and he has made me understand that my atitude towards you was wrong. He explained how I should of known better, and I aggree with him.

Please forgive my truely awfull behaviour in your excellent classes (which I really do enjoy), and I promise to show you all the respect I now know you deserve.

Yours full of regrets and remorse

Priam Hardy

```
X-ViruChekked: Checked
From: Hip@stcretiens.org.uk
Date: Mon, 19 Feb 2010 12:55:08 EST
Subject: sanctions at St. Cretien's
To: royandbrenda@yahoo.co.uk
X-Mailer: CompuServ 2001 6.0 for Windeyes UK sub 233309
X-MD-d: elliehopes@s-herald.org.uk
X-Return-Path: hip@school@stcretiens.org.uk
Reply-To: hip@school@stcretiens.org.uk
```

elliehopes@s-herald.org.uk

Dear Ellie,

Great to see you again yesterday. I hope you got back safely. What a good show the place put on! Since then things have become even more surreal. Apparently there is to be a rather important royal visitor at some point in 2012, though no-one is supposed to know about it. Needless to say it was my Fifth Form who informed me!

The boy Priam Hardy who has been such a pain in the backside this term in my German lessons has managed to offend not only me but also our assistant from Berlin, Inge Schloggenfeuerhauer who he referred to as Fraulein Shag-for-hours in a junior debate at the weekend. Unbelievably, his House Master sees fit normally to give him merely early beds as a punishment, i.e. 10.30!

What finally caused him to get a letter home was his use of the school internet to download a number of photographs which apparently brought tears to the Second Master's eyes. However, I tested the waters with the Hardy child and found that in fact his punishment from the House Master was to tidy his room and then to help serve some guests of his at the weekend, for which he had the reward of getting hammered at the expense of the school. I look forward to meeting some truly unfortunate parents next month at Parents' Evening...

Hopefully we'll meet up again at the weekend? I'm looking forward to an evening away from this place - it does tie you up completely for days and weeks on end, and sometimes I don't get out into the real world for ages! But it was good to get together last week with your friends on the Herald, they were great fun. I must say, I hope they can be discreet about their sources!

How would you like to get away completely in the Half Term? I was thinking we might actually go somewhere, maybe for a couple of days? I was wondering if you fancied going over to France, maybe even Paris?...

Lots of love,

Henry

THE ST. CRETIEN'S

DEBATING SOCIETY

Please join us in the Library for this week's debate,
followed by tea, coffee and biscuits

This week's motion:

THIS HOUSE BELIEVES THAT SCIENTOLOGISTS NEED THEIR HEADS SEEING TO

*

Thursday, 7.30 pm

Please ensure you obtain your Housemaster's / Housemistress'
permission beforehand

[154]

SCHOOL OFFICE MEMORANDUM – COMMON ROOM NOTICE BOARD

<u>Saturday Evening Detentions</u>   20 . 2 . 10

Tess Coe	single	Dominating presence in High Street on a trip
Zayne Sperries	double	Wearing a dreadful uniform
Priam Hardy	single	Killing a cat
Rose Waite	single	Having tastes too expensive for the school
Gillian Querty	single	Smoking
George Humphrey	single	Ordering kebabs on a Tuesday
Toby Frucker	single	Impersonating a member of staff
Summer Fields	single	Going over to the local Co-op without permission
Budd Jenns	single	Found unexpectedly at the local petrol station
Rachel Yell	single	Flirting with grounds staff
Eleanor Filler	single	Smoking
Morris Honns	double	Turning up where least expected
Hyacinthe Redoubt	single	Stealing sulphuric acid from labs
Graham Graham	single	Heckling in Chapel
Copra Tivv	single	Being uncooperative
Oscar Uncthorpe	single	Smoking in cinema visit
Frederick Sallyhope	single	Indescribable events on the School Farm
Al Dee	single	Cutting corners to make savings
Trevor Hui-Yang	double	Missing periods 7 & 8, Friday
Francesca Ringround	single	Scurrilous poem in the School Magazine
Nathan McEvans	double	Failure to cease self abuse when requested
Bee Jammes	single	Going over to Iceland without permission

All detentions will take place in **TMM's room** (Science 9) from 7.30 pm till 10.00
Entrance to disco thereafter will be left to House Parent's discretion, case by case.

```
X-ViruChekked: Checked
From: afg@stcretiens.org.uk
Date: Mon, 22 Feb 2010 12:17:09 EST
Subject: Sonja Mangle's Afternoon Clubs
To: Pig@stcretiens.org.uk
X-Mailer: CompuServ 2001 6.0 for Windeyes UK sub 233309
X-MD-d: Afg@school.mail
X-Return-Path: afg@school@stcretiens.org.uk
Reply-To: afg@school@stcretiens.org.uk
```

afg@stcretiens.org.uk

Re: Sonja Mangle's Afternoon Clubs

Dear Peregrine,

Just a bit worried now about certain activities in the Science Block Room 13. As I am sure you are aware, Sonja Mangle runs a number of different activities/workshops every Thursday. Recently, as a Housemaster reading out notices to the whole House in Roll Call, I have been aware of a developing trend towards increasingly anti-semitic talks/debates, which have upset the Jewish contingent in Deeping House.

Last term she held a discussion forum regarding the way that the "so-called Chosen People have squandered their good start in history through a series of heinous crimes against the rest of humanity" and has now followed it with one entitled, "How can we justify the great error of creating an independent Jewish Homeland?" Louis Goldberg, from the Lower Sixth, even went along, partly to protest, but he ended up being hounded out by a whole crowd, apparently whipped up into a frenzy by Sonja.

Please could you investigate further? Louis is a pleasant boy, and is quite shaken by it all.

Hope you can shed some light on the matter.

Thanks,

Andrew.

WELTING HOUSE

Mr. Barry Kuller

To: PIG   Date: 24:02:10

Re: Harold Price & Ryan Dumpling, Third Form

Peregrine,
       I am referring this case to you after a particularly nasty event yesterday afternoon, when two of my boys stepped severely over the mark in the House. I came back from hockey practice, rather exhausted form a long day, and found the two boys in the TV Room at 4.45.

       As you may or may not know, I insist that anybody watching TV between 4.30pm and 5.00pm must be tuned in to Channel Four's quiz show, Countdown, which I feel is educational and entertaining to boot (Not as much as Fifteen-To-One used to be, but there we go...). These boys were watching something mindless on another channel, and when I challenged them about this, they protested that they had turned over during the commercial break. Meanwhile, back on Channel Four, Countdown was in full swing, suggesting either dishonesty or negligence on their part.

       I do admit I reacted with some vehemence when they responded with their lame excuses, and when one of the boys cried through his mock-tears that he wanted to phone his mother, I am afraid to confess I almost lashed out at him. I then said he had better indeed phone his mother, from my office, to tell her that she had better come to pick him up, as he was now likely to be facing expulsion.

       On reflection, I am sure that permanent exclusion is too simplistic an answer to this particular case, and perhaps you could talk some sense into them, and emphasise how important the underlying principle is here. As a House Master now of some fourteen years, I am not accustomed to such insubordination from thirteen-year-olds; all the boys in Welting House are aware of the rules I have here, and know that I insist on their abiding by the House rules, regardless of what they claim goes on in other houses. I am quite ready to relinquish these boys, if you feel that a house change is appropriate, given their inability to play by the rules in this one.

       Thank-you for looking into this.

Cheers!

The Master's Lodge,
Sedgwickham,
West Sussex,

24th Feb, 2010

There is to be an emergency Head Master's Assembly this evening at 7.30 in Grand Hall, to which everybody, staff and pupils, is required to attend. Please be prompt, be in school uniform, and enter the Hall as quietly as possible.

The matter in hand is of the utmost importance, and therefore mobile phones must be turned off, and the Third and Fourth Form should furthermore come blindfolded, until such time as it is appropriate for them to witness the atrocities.

A. K. Warble

ALAN WARBLE, BA CANTAB, Dip Ed

MEMORANDUM from the Second Master

DATE: 24 :02 :10   **RE:** Hoax Notices

Please note that a spate of hoax notices, allegedly originating from the Head, have been circulating around the School. It is believed that a group of Upper VI may be responsible, but we cannot pin it down yet. Please remain vigilant, remove any offending materials you happen upon from public places and hand anything you find on to me.

Thank-you to everyone who turned up for the hoax assembly, and in particular to those who tried to maintain the requested silence. I am sorry that some amongst our Third and Fourth Formers suffered minor injuries when, unable to see, they fell *en masse* down the steps outside Grand Hall, and I am grateful to the Infirmary Nurse for taking the twelve pupils who ended up with fractures to Accident and Emergency, and staying with them all through the night.

24. 02. 10: PIG

School office memorandum – Common room notice board

<u>Saturday Evening Detentions   27 . 02 . 10</u>

Abby Rhode	single	Climbing on a roof
Eleanor Rigby	single	Taking someone else's rice
Polly (Pam) Theen	single	Climbing in through bathroom window
Johnny Goode	single	Twisting things
Letty Bee	single	Promising too much
Robert Saul	single	Driving a car
Rhea Vulva	single	Only sleeping
Pippa Sargeaunt	single	Laughing loudly while reading newspaper
Martin George	single	Giving a little too much help to his friends
Priam Hardy	double	Never knowing his natural boundaries
Sheila Vessiou	single	Shouting "yeah" repeatedly
Max Well	single	Using a hammer inappropriately
Lucy Diamond	single	Being out after bedtime to look at stars
Madge Ickle	double	Getting on a bus without permission
Miss Terry Torre	single	Eating too many noodles
Sadie Yxès	single	Making a fool of everyone; breaking all rules
Andi Lover	double	Spoiling a perfectly good party
Ian Walrus	single	Keeping eggs in his room
Lizzy Dizzy	single	Dancing frenetically
Glayze O'Nyon	double	Pretending a former friend was dead
Maggie May	single	Getting on the train to Liverpool
Penny Laine	single	Standing in the middle of a roundabout
Tristan Showte	double	Being very loud and very annoying

All detentions will take place in **TMM's room** (Science 9) from 7.30 pm till 10.00
Entrance to disco thereafter will be left to House Parent's discretion, case by case.

```
X-ViruChekked: Checked
From: Puf@stcretiens.org.uk
Date: Mon, 01 March 2010 09:45:22 EST
Subject: Cedric Gunter's art work
To: Daf@stcretiens.org.uk
X-Mailer: CompuServ 2001 6.0 for Windeyes UK sub 233309
X-MD-d: Daf@school.mail
X-Return-Path: Puf@school@stcretiens.org.uk
Reply-To: Puf@school@stcretiens.org.uk
```

daf@stcretiens.org.uk

Dear Daffyd,

As Cedric Gunter's House Master, I know you'll be as worried as I am
regarding his recent project in art. As a whole year group, the Fifth
Form are beginning the second stage of their coursework, and Cedric has
approached this with plenty of gusto, as you can well imagine. I believe
Cedric to be a creative young man, and am sure that he will thrive if he
goes on to study art at college, as he hopes to. However, I am very
shocked by his choice of material for this particular topic.

We gave them the title "Earth and Earthiness" in the hope of them
producing still-lifes of flowers, studies of the texture of landscapes,
maybe even something touching on modern-day concerns for our environment.
Sally Rhys has produced some excellent "Gaia"-themed work.

However, Sandra Grate, Cedric's teacher this year,tells me he has spent a
good three or four lessons now smearing canvases with what can only be
described as excrement, not all of it non-human, I might add. The other
pupils are both appalled and fascinated as he arrives each lesson with
various carrier-bags full of different types of faeces. The effects of
contrasting colours are admittedly quite striking, but I am very worried
indeed about where he is acquiring all this filth, and how he is handling
it. In the workshop, he makes quite a mess, and eschews traditional
brushes and knives.

Not only is Barry from Health and Safety going to rightly kick up a stink
when he discovers this, but it really is beginning to reek down here, and
I really cannot take prospective parents around without feeling
embarrassed; only last week, the son of visiting parents vomited all over
one of Sally Rhys' "Gaia" watercolours, and I didn't know where to look.
Sandra is also becoming rather tired of it all.

Please could you have a word with him about this, see if he could do
something on fields and crops and hibernating animals, etc.

Thanks!

Petra

Ms. Grate
(a very grate artist!)

The Master's Lodge,
Sedgwickham,
West Sussex,

1st March, 2010

In response to a growing problem of acute homelessness in the town, St. Cretien's will be opening its doors to a number of down-and-outs, who will be put up in empty boys' rooms, and who will play a full rôle in the life of the School.

Naturally, we would expect any tramps who do take up the offer to play a full part in daily life, and their presence would be very welcome indeed at Chapel, morning assemblies, meal-times and perhaps doing a weekly evening duty in a boarding house, keeping an eye on prep-times, lock-ups and putting the pupils to bed.

Any incidence of illicit drinking or smoking of illegal substances or otherwise would, of course, be severely reprimanded, but it would be hoped that the School would be offering in the longer term some sort of a local service to our community, in a sense putting something back into society.

Not only is it planned in the longer term to be able to include their numbers on the school roll, so as to boost our size officially, but it is also hoped to be able to persuade the district council to contribute to the maintenance costs.

We will kick off the whole project with a special *GRAB A TRAMP* run into town, this Saturday 6th, to recruit a number of our first group of inmates.

A. K. Wobble

ALAN WOBBLE, BA CANTABury, Dip Ed

The Master's Lodge,
Sedgwickham,
West Sussex,

2nd March, 2010

A bring-and-buy is to take place next Saturday afternoon in aid of Dr. Farouk's Islamicist Fanatics Fund. Please contribute generously and encourage as many friends and associates to come and look around.

Mr. B.O. Killer will be responsible for the stall selling maternity wear and toddlers clothing
Mr. S.T. Disease is kindly helping out with the knitwear stall
Mr. P.I. Grueson and Mrs. D.U. Dragoon are in charge of the Anne Summers stalls
Dr. E.F. Fuller will take care of the tombola (prize: a meal at a top local restaurant with the Head and Mrs. Wobble)
Mr. T.P. Samuels will be helping to serve fairy cakes

Please promote this event as much as you all can.

A. K. Wobble

ALAN WOBBLE, BA CANTAB, Dip Head

P255677:wrm2

11/03/10

45a\ref.114
CRNB

ST. CRETIEN'S COLLEGE
WORKS AND MAINTENANCE DEPT.

Re: H&S Directive 41850:6 (f) – Health and Safety Working Committee (HSWC)

Advance notice is hereby given regarding the implementation of H&S Directive 41850:6 (f) in accordance with EU Regulations 335 & 762 of 1996 Commission Report and File 56, pertaining to speed of local traffic on private land.

It has been brought to the attention of the HSWC by recent investigation undertaken by Barry that a number of resident members of staff drive around the site in a fashion which irresponsibly puts all members of the St. Cretien's community at risk, most of all the pupils and those disabled who fail to move fast enough. With these groups as ever foremost in mind, we have consulted with the SMT and have agreed to implement a new speed restriction of 5 mph across the overall site, and down to 2 mph within the central area around the Quad.

This will be enforced at first by Barry and myself, though it is very likely that in due course a number of discreet speed cameras may well have to be installed at pivotal places within the school, should the intransigence of certain members of staff continue to put everybody's lives at risk. As ever, of course, it is the few who spoil it for the many.

Thank-you for your support in helping St. Cretien's community help itself.

Brian Blouse, GWTO, c/o HSWC

BB : 11/03/10

The Master's Lodge,
Sedgwickham,
West Sussex,

12th March, 2010

If any staff or members of the Upper Sixth would like to book one or a number of call-girls for events or private use, please contact the Director of Studies, Mr. Anthony Ingham on 07778 9455742455 between 9.30pm and 3.00am.

A. K. Wobble

ALAN WOBBLE, BA CANTAB, Dip Ed

School office memorandum – Common room notice board

Saturday Evening Detentions   13 . 3 . 10

Labbo Hemm	single	Having a very untidy room
Don Jivani	double	Throwing wild oats all over the school
Cosipha Tooty	double	Dressing up in someone else's clothes
Priam Hardy	single	Spitting at visiting clergy
Harry Dercules	single	Correcting members of staff
Jeremy Springer	single	Offending the Chaplain with profanities
Geoffrey Salad	single	Behaviour
Oscar Uncthorpe	single	Smoking in Headmaster's Assembly
Dan Hoyser	double	Singing competitively loudly in his room
Jennifer Thwaite	single	Smoking
Gillian Querty	single	Smoking
Barbara Seville	single	Too complicated to explain
Frederick Sallyhope	single	Refusal to face facts about animals
Ada Carman	single	Getting seduced by an Egyptian gypsy
Dwain Kirkby	single	Defacing the Head's portrait in Dining Hall
Flynn Hollander	single	Taking out a rowing boat and refusing to return
Eleanor Filler	single	Smoking
Benjamin Stroke	double	Encouraging juniors to drink
Madge Hickflute	double	Instigating silly handshakes all round school
Trevor Hui-Yang	double	Missing periods 5 & 6, Monday
Boris Goodenough	double	Pretending to be Russian to a visiting teacher

All detentions will take place in **TMM's room** (Science 9) from 7.30 pm till 10.00
Entrance to disco thereafter will be left to House Parent's discretion, case by case.

SATURDAY EVENING
STAFF DUTY PATROL REPORT

Date: _13/3/10_

Duty Team Leader: _Tony Adonals_

Duty Team: _SUI, SRA_

An evening in which sheer military might and strategic thinking outmatched and outflanked all potential shenanigans by the troops! We were a crack team, our squadron of Selwyn and Sally, and we fought off every offensive by the enemy until they withdrew in defeat.

Early evening circa 20 hundred hours a few individuals were seen to be heading off to Underwood Lane for an illicit smoke, so we flushed them out with a double pincer strike, similar to Monty's famous advance attack at El Alamein. All five boys summarily admonished and sent back to House with a buzzing flea in their ears. Similar incident later with one of the very same boys, and this time I gave him merry hell.

At 21 hundred hours we convened onto our elevated position above the swimming pool and observed the enemy's wider movements without being seen ourselves, then, synchronizing our chronometers, we stole into the range of thickets behind Jeville Block, and surprised a group of Fourth to Sixth Formers all enjoying a substance akin to Marijuana, which Selwyn confiscated and promised to hide in his office in the Drama Dept. I sent the offending criminals straight to the senior House Master on Duty.

The School Disco tonight was themed around the military, which I am afraid merely egged on my killer instincts even more, and I shall detail PIG in the morning about some of the accidents which occurred during the horse play some of the seniors brought upon themselves.

By 23 hundred hours all was very quiet on the Western Front, and my team and I felt there was no more to do. I invited them for a little schnoofter in the bar, but Sally had to get home to her husband, and Selwyn said he had some work to finish off in his office, so I retired there myself, and was glad to join some of the young turks who had already started enjoying their Saturday evening, but who also left soon after.

23.45: Wrote up this report.

                                                                    TGA

Thanks Tony for all the hard work !

                                                    Peregrine

MEMORANDUM from the Second Master

DATE: 15 :03 :10   **RE:**   Master's Cloakroom

I should like to remind our male colleagues that the CR cleaners do a truly sterling job for all of us, and I am sure you would be more than happy to help in any way at all to lighten their daily load.

Our Senior Cleaner, Jean, has brought it to my attention that of all the urinals in the male cloakroom, the second urinal on the left is constantly the dirtiest by far, and therefore the most difficult to maintain, whilst the two or three furthest urinals often remain spotless.

Of course, we are all prone to our little habits, and I am sure we all just aim straight for the second urinal out of sheer convenience and speed (for any ladies illegally reading this, the first urinal on the left is too far up against the near wall and quite awkward to use, especially for gentlemen with wide elbows), but I would ask you from now on to make a special effort on your next visit to the lavatory to be more attentive as to the distribution of your urinal usage, and perhaps then to monitor the overall frequency with which you use certain ones.

With care and a little consideration, we ought to avoid the continued build-up we've seen of unsightly residue due simply to overuse.

Thank-you for your help.

15/03/10: PIG

Peregrine,

Does this count for number one's only ? Should I revise

my whole policy now for number two's ?

[169]

MEMORANDUM from the Second Master

DATE: 16 :02 :10   **RE:** Master's Cloakroom

There is no excuse for colleagues to deface CRNB notices, and if anyone should have any serious queries or comments, they should address them to me personally, and I shall do my utmost, as you know, to deal with whatever issues are raised.

Important notices are not pinned to the CRNB simply for cheap laughs.

Thank-you

16/02/10: PIG

Mr. Geoffrey
Bernay

The Master's Lodge,
Sedgwickham,
West Sussex,

17th March, 2010

Members of staff will be shocked and saddened to learn of the death of Mr. Geoffrey J. Bernay, who passed away peacefully and unnoticed in the Lent Term of 1954, yet who has managed to keep on working well beyond this untimely end, and indeed has admirably continued teaching Classics with exactly the same energy and success as he did in life. On behalf of the Common Room, I have passed on our deepest condolences to his widow, who was as shocked as we were to learn of his demise.

A. K. Wobble

ALAN WOBBLE, BA COLDTAP, Dip Ed

The Master's Lodge,
Sedgwickham,
West Sussex,

19th March, 2010

Before addressing a press conference, the Head Master has decided to announce to the Common Room and pupils of St. Cretien's his personal joy and relief since resolving to out himself; he would like everyone to know he is not a human, but is in fact a rare form of extra-terrestrial life that has existed on Earth since before the coming of the dinosaurs, and who is imbued with all the wisdom of a minor God. Henceforth he shall be addressed as Alpha, the nearest rendering of his name in the crude Earthling tongue.

He will be happy to take any questions on his decision during Head Master's Assembly (now to be renamed "Audience with Alpha"), and trusts that none of this will impact significantly on everyday school life.

Alpha K. Wobble

ALPHA WOBBLE, BA KRPYTON, Pluto, Big Dipper

The Master's Lodge,
Sedgwickham,
West Sussex,

20th March, 2010

As the School has at last accepted the need for an official Smoking Spot, and made the Underwood Lane the place it always was, I have decided to designate Scanker's House the official place for pupils to go who absolutely must have sex with one another (or alone, in the case of Harry Terence).

Scanker's House will be renamed Bonkers' House, after a former House Captain, and will be open at all times apart from prep-time and Wednesday afternoons, so as not to interfere with Community Service programmes. I would like to add my personal thanks to Mrs. Fiona Derry, who has kindly agreed to take over as House Mistress.

Alpha K. Wobble

ALPHA WOBBLE, BA CANTABury, Dip Ed

The St. Cretien's

Christian Union

is meetin' next thurs

7.30pm

in the

Chapel Crypt

Subject: "Why we so

RIGHT when we

got THE LORD ?"

bthere or
bsquare!!!

ST. CRETIEN'S COLLEGE
WEST SUSSEX

From the Inspection Enforcement Officer

Level: 4A:Inspection (urgent)/5B:Ongoing (urgent) Code: «9004-6337»
Marking and Assessment [sec. 8.5 & 8.6]
HBGR-721(b) 20th March, 2010

Re: The Inspection, April 19th-21st, 2010

As I am sure you are all well aware, St. Cretien's is intending to undergo an TOFFSTED Inspection next month. In the final weeks, however, there are still a few loose ends to tie up, including the awkward, but very crucial, issue of staff dress.

Let me begin by saying that the staff at St. Cretien's are by and large sartorially conversant as regards how they dress for lessons. But unfortunately, there are instances now and again of inappropriate items of clothing being employed. Below is an outline of what the SMT expects of staff dress on a day-to-day basis.

- Gentlemen should wear sober, semi-formal clothes, preferably suits, but without the kind of modern cut associated with fashionable City wide-boys.
- Ladies should wear smart dress, either skirts/dresses or trousers, though SMT do have a preference for something that shows the legs. However, the line must be drawn at anything that borders on "skimpy" or "slutty," and must certainly not draw attention to the breasts – or legs, for that matter.
- Bow-ties and elbow patches should rightly be reserved for male members of the Latin/History Departments only.
- No gowns, please, except for formal occasions; on such occasions, please can we have only sober/serious-coloured gowns, as some of the more gaudy, garish ones, especially from universities across the Atlantic, can look a little loud and frivolous here in an old school like St. Cretien's.
- Would ladies in particular be careful as to what shoes they choose to wear. Again, stylish with a hint of "sassy" is what I reckon most of my male colleagues would consider the right mix, but please be aware of what impressions we give out to both the pupils and outside visitors; too much heel can quickly become suggestive, and even aggressively sexual, whilst wearing flatties every day can swiftly start to look downright frumpy.

Please feel free to speak to me, if you have any queries about this new policy.
Yours in appreciation,

Thomas Horngold

"A UNIQUE OPPORTUNITY" FOR ALL AGES!!!

Fräulein MANGLE IS RUNNING AN INFORMAL

EMBALMING WORKSHOP

ALL ARE WELCOME,
COME TO THE ROOM 13
THURSDAY 4.00 P.M.

BIOLOGY DEPARTM.,
SC.BUILDG

no specialist equipment

needed, just PLENTY of

enthusiastic, healthy bodies!

SNM

Miss Sonja Mangle at one of her
afternoon clubs

X-ViruChekked: Checked
From: Hip@stcretiens.org.uk
Date: Tue, 22 Mar 2010 11:24:11 EST
Subject: Timmy!
To: elliehopes@s-herald.org.uk
X-Mailer: CompuServ 2001 6.0 for Windeyes UK sub 233309
X-MD-d: elliehopes@s-herald.org.uk
X-Return-Path: hip@school@stcretiens.org.uk
Reply-To: hip@school@stcretiens.org.uk

elliehopes@s-herald.org.uk

Dear Ellie,

Good to meet up last week. Really enjoyed spending a bit of time with
you. Loved your article in this Saturday's edition, didn't realise there
was so much to know about whelks!

Sorry I didn't come over this weekend, but I had a couple of colleagues
around for drinks, and spent a truly hilarious evening learning all sorts
of gossip. And there is even better news than yours, I'm afraid.

Our fine, upstanding Director of Studies is fantastic with a couple of
tipples inside him, and last night was very much on form. It turns out
that a number of parents now are making complaints about the sheer
hysterical terror a certain member of the school is causing them, and I'm
not talking about Pig or even Tony Adanoids.

Apparently, a few times now, the sight of a fully grown tarantula spider
above their beds in junior dorms has sent some of the girls in Crawling
House into orbit, and rumour has it that little Samantha Piles was woken
up with it in her mouth. Dear old Timmy has been surviving perfectly well
up there near the warmth of the hot water tanks. More than just
surviving, though, so it turns out...

Clearly, even worse is yet to come! He revealed that the experts called
in to track down our resident arachnid believe him not to be a Timmy at
all, but a female! Apparently the experts have already located an
enormous egg sac hanging in the rafters, completely empty, of course...
So it looks like there's a growing community of baby tarantulas in the
nooks and crannies of the two girls' houses!

Keep watching this space.

See you next week.

Henry

[179]

Dear all, Shelly and Frank's little boy, Justin, is doing wonderfully, and we're all delighted with the extra little bit of distraction. We're all a little worried because our captors are trying to teach us how to use Kalashnikovs etc, and I think they've already got their eye on Justin being a child-spy once he's old enough to walk, to take over from their suicide-bomber monkeys, which are wholly unreliable (one went off last week in the middle of one of Pat's flower-arranging classes, and ruined the whole atmosphere, as well as a wonderful display of wild orchids which would have cheered up the place no end). Tim (et al)

The Common Room,
St. Cretien's Coll.,
Sedgwickham,
West Sussex,
Inghiliterra.

(TMM)

PLEASE WOULD YOU COVER THE FOLLOWING LESSON FOR: GAF

PERIOD: 5   DAY: Mon   DATE: 22nd March

MANY THANKS.

Timothy,

Cheers for covering this Fourth Form class. They have just moved on to the next section of my worksheets, which may be a little taxing for the weaker ones, but it's nothing new – we discussed what the Enlightenment was last lesson, and how useful it can be to learn the language through these writers, so just see what you can do to help them on their way. It's nothing too specialised as yet, just some basic Lessing and Kant, much of which we've talked about already. However, anything you can contribute would be great!

For those who finish translating the opening chapter of the Kritik der reinen Vernunft, they can move on to the next part, which is an essay on the importance of Lessing's interpretation of the Laocoön.

Prep is learn the forty words and phrases on p. 26 of their Deutsch Heute books about how to order train-tickets.

Thanks again for covering them,

Gary

P255677:wrm2

22/03/10

45a\ref.166
CRNB

ST. CRETIEN'S COLLEGE
WORKS AND MAINTENANCE DEPT.

Re: H&S Directive 42339:16 (f) – Health and Safety Working Committee (HSWC)

At the weekend, a serious incident occurred in the Theatre, when the grand piano, normally resident on stage, was discovered to have a faulty joint in its nearside front leg, a fault which was only discovered during one of Brian's weekly instrument inspections. This was immediately identified by Brian as a situation which could potentially lead to fatalities, should anybody be rash enough to be playing the instrument in an unorthodox manner, or indeed if the player were to have assumed an awkward position due to some permanent disability. As it is our foremost responsibility to protect the pupils and staff here, especially the disabled, it was felt by the HSWC to require urgent attention, and has led therefore to the establishment of the current restrictions in the Theatre.

The aforementioned piano (a "Stienway", which we are reliably informed is a make not normally associated with such structural defects) was immediately declared unfit for purpose, and the entire stage has been designated as an official "DEMARCATED ZONE". This means that there is to remain in place, until such notification as is released by the HSWC, effectively a no-go area to both staff and pupils; exception has been made, however, for the cleaner, Mrs. Serena Huang-King, who is lucky to be working here at all, given her lack of accredited National Insurance contributions.

In the meantime, with the helpful assistance of Security, a safety cage has been constructed around the aforementioned piano, and the whole stage has been cordoned off with tape (sorry that it reads "Murder Inquiry", but that's all the police could spare for this month!). It is hoped that any pupil who is troublesome enough to interfere with this safety cage would be dealt with most severely by staff; furthermore, may the HSWC make the recommendation that any members of staff who contravene the restrictions of the Demarcation Zone should be prepared to face the very real prospect of a Citizen's Arrest administered by Security

I trust that the present situation with the Stenierway piano will be appreciated as unacceptable in every sense, and all our efforts will be fully supported by staff and pupils alike. Mindful of this weeks' rehearsal's for next Saturday's musical "The Piano Man" , we can only apologise about the current impasse, and regret the two months delay which full repairs will entail. Clearly we are making every effort possible to get the stage back to normal as soon as we can, but it will be understood, I hope, that Health and Safety concerns for the wellbeing of our community here come first and foremost in our minds.

Thank-you all for your cooperation.

Barry Soddum, GWTO, c/o HSWC

BS : 22/03/10

School office memorandum – Common room notice board

<u>Saturday Evening Detentions</u>   27 . 3 . 10

Andy Popakata	single	Climbing too high on School Tower
Chomolungma Everest	single	Deliberately making people feel dizzy
Kay Too	single	Not being happy with second-best
Priam Hardy	single	Inability to turn over a new leaf in History
Eleanor Filler	single	Smoking
Vee Zuvios	single	Covering his whole room in ash after smoking
Kyle Ash	single	Having everyone run rings round him
Geoffrey Salad	single	Behaviour
Edna Crackatoe	double	Having an explosive temper
Harry Dercules	single	Smoking
Jennifer Thwaite	single	Smoking
Himmle Ayers	double	Acting aloof
Priam Hardy	single	Theft of materials from Chemistry
Trevor Hui-Yang	double	Missing Wednesday entirely
Benjamin Knevis	single	Stormy behaviour
Oscar Uncthorpe	single	Smoking at swimming gala
Graham Graham	single	Threatening to burn Chaplain at the stake
Matt O'Horne	single	Claiming neighbour to be a virgin
Vaughan Smiler	single	Picking flowers from the Quad
Frederick Sallyhope	single	Guess!
Skaffil Pyke	single	Never having anything to show for so much work
Steven Orral	single	Mooning at prospective parents

All detentions will take place in **TMM's room** (Science 9) from 7.30 pm till 10.00
Entrance to disco thereafter will be left to House Parent's discretion, case by case.

P255677:wrm2

29/3/10

56d\ref.388
CRNB

ST. CRETIEN'S COLLEGE
WORKS AND MAINTENANCE DEPT.

Re: H&S Directive 41798:5 (e) – Health and Safety Working Committee (HSWC)

Advance notice is hereby given concerning the implementation of H&S Directive 43347:5 (f) in accordance with EU Regulations 221 & 890 of 1998 Commission Report and File 22, pertaining to the risk assessment of vehicular speed on the sites where children are either fully or partially resident.

It has been brought to me and Barry's attention that, despite a genuine attempt on our part to raise colleagues' awareness of the dangers of speeding on site, a number of staff and visitors continue to scoff at the restrictions agreed upon and now in place, with the result that in the last month alone we have recorded a depressing nineteen potential "near-misses" (as defined in the UK Aviation Code 2002). We feel therefore, given the looming Inspection, and the need to comply with relevant regulations, that this is something which needed to be tackled with some urgency.

We dread to think how many similar events have actually occurred and gone unreported, so it is in the light of this that we have overseen the erection of a large number of signs around the site, intended to ward all drivers away from the evils of complacency when behind the wheel. The signs will light up in neon whenever a vehicle approaches, and emit a sudden, sharp audio signal as a warning; our apologies to anyone who lives in proximity to one of these new "Audio Battery Assisted Warning Visual Signals" but after all, they are for the good of the entire community.

The wording on the signs will be in bold capitals, and will contain one of the following messages to any wayward driver:

- ST. CRETIEN'S CHILDREN VERY SLOW

- SLOWER CHILDREN AHEAD

- DEAD SLOW CHILDREN HERE

- ABANDON ALL SPEED YE WHO ENTER HERE

- BRAKE DON'T BREAK!

- THE ONLY POINTS YOU GET FOR MAIMING A CRETIAN WILL BE ON YOUR LICENCE

- BREAKING THE LIMITS? SHAME ON YOU

Thank-you all for your support.

Brian Blouse, GWTO, c/o HSWC

BB : 29/3/10

ST. CRETIEN'S COLLEGE
WEST SUSSEX

From the Inspection Enforcement Officer

Level: 4A:Inspection (urgent)/5B:Ongoing (urgent)   Code: «3332-8466»
CRB Checks [sec. 3.3 & 3.4]
HBGR-557(f)   29th March, 2010

IMPORTANT NOTICE – PLEASE READ CAREFULLY

ADVANCE NOTICE: TEMPORARY EXTENSION OF THE END OF LENT TERM

As some of you have already no doubt heard, this unavoidable and unprecedented move is largely in response to a systemic failure in the Risk Assessment Schedule, re. "Extended Leave and Holidays [sections. 3.3 & 3.4]," and is due to a regrettable oversight on the part of the St. Cretien's Health and Safety Executive Committee (SCHASEC).

It is therefore with reluctance that we are obliged to postpone **at least the beginning** of the coming Easter Holidays. Unfortunately, this will require **all current staff** to stay on site for a number of days after the weekend of 3rd – 4th April, and over the Easter period, in order to manage and supervise the pupils, in an attempt to ensure that all eventualities have been covered in the run-up to the Inspection (which is happening, incidentally, this coming April).

It was brought to the school's attention at last night's HSEC meeting that if we were to send our pupils home on the 2nd April, as published in the Calendar, then there are a number of very grave risks for which the school could be considered liable. First and foremost is the inexcusable fact that an <u>overwhelming majority</u> of our parents have not had even the most basic type of CRB check, and we could thus easily be sending some of our pupils into desperately unpalatable situations, and at least five of them to almost certain death. For this reason alone there is to be expected a turnaround of about seven days, before we receive the required CRB results, and are able to proceed with further steps towards rehabilitation.

There were also a number of related concerns which were raised at the meeting:

- Untold numbers of parents are still not yet fully trained with compliant school driving standards, and this could pose serious threats to life and limb during a period when families tend to take potentially lethal motor vehicles for days-out and excursions.

- It may be fairly assumed that a small number of even our pupils go home to so-called high-rise blocks of flats, many of which are still without safety features for stopping windows from opening more than 1.5cm. Only when St. Cretien's own designated Openings & Orifices Tsar (Brian Blouse) has checked off each relevant property (and at the same time done a routine check for active paedophiles in the area) can we let our pupils back into these buildings.

- There is at present a real and ongoing threat from Somali pirates, who have been operating from bases as close as Boosaaso, Bircao and Bexhill. A tiny number of our children also have some shady family links with places in Africa, which should make us all doubly aware of this danger.

- Finally, in a further measure to stem a potential Swine Fever epidemic within the school, Underwood Gate will be closed indefinitely.

Knowing that you know that we know better.

Yours in appreciation,

Thomas Horngold

Hello, all! Phew! It's been a jolly testing time for us all, but awfully exciting too! We've now been taken by another group, God only knows who, and we're holed up in a mountain hideaway somewhere, with a huge ransom on our heads and the threat of summary executions for every two weeks that pass, but don't worry, I don't think it's you at St Cretien's who they're demanding it from! Still, I'm not sure if C-Room funds would stretch that far, given what I remember of its finances! Anyway, we reckon they're bluffing!! Thought you'd like the picture on this postcard; Jose Barillas is a local pop star, but he's the spitting image of the old Bursar, isn't he! Yours, *Tim*

The Common Room,
St. Cretien's Coll.,
Sedgwickham,
West Sussex,
Inghiliterra.

[187]

Hawthorn Towers,
The Wold

Easter 2010

Dear Mr. & Mrs. Farrow,

Hope you like these truffles, we always find them very tasty indeed! Have an excellent holiday, and make sure you take these and the hamper with you!

We were glad to hear of your intervention in getting the school to see sense, and not to stay open any longer than need be! We heard you were rather vocal, and we can't blame you, though we must admit we had been quite excited when we learned that Priam might not be coming home for a while... Never mind!

Once again, thank-you in particular for your concern and your care in dealing with Priam's occasional lapses this term. We feel sure he has turned a corner now, and we know for a fact he is determined to pay you back for your time and effort. In the meantime, we trust you will accept our little token as our thanks!

All the best!

The Hardys

SUMMER TERM

April, 2010

ST. CRETIEN'S COLLEGE
WEST SUSSEX

From the Inspection Enforcement Officer

Level: 4A:Inspection (urgent)/5B:Ongoing (urgent)   Code: «9004-6337»
Marking and Assessment [sec. 8.5 & 8.6] and all other sections
HBGR-721(b)   7th April, 2010

Re: The Inspection, April 19th – 21st, 2012

The names of the team for the coming Inspection has been released to us, and I must say, it's a pretty high-brow group of individuals coming here to look us over. There are five Inspectors in total, coming from a variety of Independent Schools across the country, and include two specialists in human behavioural disorders. They'll be arriving on Sunday evening, for dinner in the Common Room, hosted by the Head Master, his wife and PIG with Mrs. Grueson, and attended by all the SMT – we had hoped to use the Head Master's House, but Barry and Brian from Health and Safety have informed us that the building is at present in no state to host such august company, which has surprised and shocked Mrs. Warble, who has since been heard to say it was in a good enough state these last twenty-five years to bring three children up in, so what's suddenly the problem now?..

The Inspection Team comprises of:

- Dr. Russ Yarwell   -   Head Master of St. Cytringan's College

- Mr. Brett Ainsworth   -   Deputy Head of St. George's Upper School

- Mr. Chai Navjoat   -   Head Teacher of St. Joseph's College

- Mrs. Fran Cyril   -   Head Mistress of St. Denis' Cloisters

- Mrs. Amery Cardell   -   Senior Master of St. Mammon's Sixth Form Sch.

All five Inspectors will be staying at the Stittstoveller Inn in Sedgwickham for the duration of their visit, and will start their work on Monday morning first thing. I need hardly point out that the impact they should have on our lessons and teaching really will be minimal, but I hope you are all aware of their timetable, as regards the lessons to be observed. As you know, over the course of the four days, each member of staff can expect to be observed at least twelve times, so I hope all those lesson plans are in place and ready to be followed!

Please feel free to speak to me, if you have any queries about all this.

Thomas Horngold

Hello. Sadly, we've had the first of our executions today, so we're all rather down. William Wolly was taken away by three guerrillas, and shot by some of the very weapons we recognised we had made at the munitions plant; it was with some satisfaction for Willy and ourselves that they kept jamming, and that it took seven attempts finally to put him out of his misery. Commiserations from us all to his family. On the plus side, one of our captors is bizarrely a fan of celebrity magazines, so we are keeping abreast of what's happening back home through past copies of OK and Hello. Well, must dash. Yours as ever, Tim et al.

The Common Room,
St. Cretien's Coll.,
Sedgwickham,
West Sussex,
Inglaterra.

ST. CRETIEN'S LIBRARY

FROM Mrs. HAGGERS
THE LIBRARIAN

02. 04. 10

Welcome back to the new term! Unfortunately, I must report my displeasure at having to chase up yet again the following books borrowed by Common Room. Please ensure that these books are returned as soon as possible! Thank-you. Might I also remind you that the life of a Librarian and Archivist is by no means the proverbial Life of Reilly everybody would have you believe. I could certainly have done without this extra layer of bureaucracy to burden my Easter Holidays.

Geoffrey Bernay	*The Nude in Photos* *Female Icons of the Cinema* *Audrey Hepburn*
Anthony Ingham	*Highlights of Americana*
Ralph Selton	*Painful Train Journeys*
Peregrine Grueson	*Where To Find Solace: Oriental Meditation* *How To Win Friends and Influence People*
Richard Pounde	*Wicca Today*
Sandra Grate	*Why Trust Men? A Survivor's Guide*
Raoul Heffer	*Art Between the Wars* *Kabarett and the Weimar Republic* *Asterix the Gaul*
Barry Kuller	*Pol Pot and the Khmer Rouge* *Staying Alive* *The Rise of the Far Right*
Steven D'Essise	*Embroidery and Cross-Stitching*
Felix Rompant	*Calibrations in Everyday Life*
Rodney Power	*Finding Your Niche* *The Power of the Female Foot*
Olivia Power	*Knowing Your Partner Completely* *Seeing the World Through The Male Psyche* *The Sceptre of Love*

GBH Apr 10

Mr. + Mrs Power – a lovely couple always together

DATES AND TIMES FOR THE START OF SUMMER TERM 2010

Monday, April 12th

9.30am	Staff Meeting in Common Room.
11.00am	Common Room Meeting in Common Room.
11.30am	Coffee Break.
12.00 noon	Short talk by Mrs Ruth Gromble:

Subject: *Finding a common path through the jargon of today's educational establishment – Securing a successful pathway to best practice!*

1.00pm	Lunch in the Dining Hall.
2.00pm	INSET Training: *Being a "Helluva Teacher" whilst maintaining integrity and discipline – notes from an old hand.*
5.00pm	Pupils begin arriving back for the start of term.
6.00pm	Dinner.
8.00pm	Roll Call in Boarding Houses.
10.30pm	Lock-up time.

Tuesday, April 13th

8.30am	Chapel for whole School.
9.30am	Lessons begin as per normal day.

04/04/10:PIG

<u>AGENDA FOR STAFF MEETING</u>

Monday, 12th April, 2010

1. Welcome Mrs. Tanya Swiller, who replaces Sylvia Welks in English, now on maternity leave

2. Head Master's business, as follows:

    *   Intention to implement compulsory Chapel every day
    *   Importance of staff not to be heard talking about the school in a negative manner
    *   Latest news on Timothy Rent
    *   Final preparations for the Inspection – at last!

3. Bursar's business, as follows:

    *   Balance of payments. General situation
    *   Fund-raising events for Summer Term
    *   Decision to use the school premises for summer school *Love Language!* Implications of having a number of foreign teenagers on site during the summer holidays
    *   The leasing out of Further Field to local farmer Reginald Bryant for seasonal grazing of sheep and occasional goats

4. Second Master's business:

    *   Behaviour in Dining Hall - especially catering staff
    *   Staff smoking patrols – a success story!
    *   Fire practices - the next is to take place on Saturday evening at 8.00; all resident staff are expected to be present and to help

5. Chaplain's business

6. Senior Master's business

7. Director of Studies
    *   Details about next week's Inspection are now posted up on the Notice Board. Many thanks indeed to Thomas Horngold, who has been instrumental in getting everything prepared for the big event, and so, over to you, Thomas!

8. Inspection Enforcement Officer's business – to be outlined in full at the meeting...

COMMON ROOM MINUTES for April, 2010

Taken by R. M. Pounde

The meeting started with a number of members of Common Room asking why the recent redecorating of the CR had to be in pastel pink with yellow curtains and yellow upholstery. MRD suggested it may be to help calm the teaching staff, whilst GRW wondered whether it was an attempt to balance out the male-female ratio of the staff, by attracting more women to what must otherwise seem quite a male club. Ms. Grate from the Art Dept said she was outraged that such petty views could even exist, never mind be aired publicly, but PIG joked (to his credit but also to his detriment) that Ms. Grate was this very day also dressed in pink, with an off-the-shoulder pastel yellow strappy thing, all topped by a turquoise scarf, but Ms. Grate screamed that this was none of his business, and furthermore irrelevant to the issue. HGE said that for his part he found the CR rather soothing now, and, if anything, it might now prove to be *too* calm an atmosphere for getting down to work, and THK from the back mentioned quietly that indeed GOB had already fallen fast asleep next to him. The President then said he would take the consensus to be on the whole positive, and he would convey the Common Room's approval of the redecoration to the Head.

The matter was then raised of annual subscription to the CR. The CR Treasurer POP stated that the CR funds were in the red, mainly because of the pay-out at the end of last academic year in presents for the twenty-nine members of staff who had to leave. He announced that the year's subscription for staff would now have to be raised to £68, in order to bring the CR back into the black. There was then much commotion amongst members of the CR. RHP wondered why we were being forced to pay more when we seemed to be getting less, and FPR agreed that with the abolition of break-time biscuits, and the change to a cheaper coffee brand, we were being heavily put-upon. HUG asked if we would be expected to drink our plebeian coffee through the nose as well paying for it through it, and BOK added that on top of all that we were also paying for the dubious privilege of meeting in our free time in a series of claustrophobic boxes painted in various sh*te, pastel colours. A number of staff then defended the colours, arguing that these were irrelevant to the argument, and that we were lucky to have had the place refurbished, as the last time it had been looked at was in early 1978.

The Treasurer POP then mooted the idea that certain newspapers and periodicals were costing the CR unnecessarily, and that maybe some of those which went relatively unread could be eliminated from the CR's subscription. Three of the younger members of CR suggested that we could reasonably do without *Holy Synod Review*, but Revd. Caustick became very vocal in his defence of this, claiming that any self-respecting master (even if still young and inexperienced) could never feel confident in an establishment like St. Cretien's without a finger on the pulse of modern theological thinking; he wondered, in fact, whether the place would be taken seriously, by prospective parents with their children's best interests at heart, were they indeed to have heard this preposterous idea even being discussed in the meeting. So the discussion was once again brought round to the perennial talk of weeding out *Country Life* from the subscription. DAF proposed this magazine finally be laid to rest, as only country people and "toffs" read it; TIT added that it also promoted fox hunting and was devoured by capitalist fascists. Ms. Grate felt that was unfair, as she found that there were plenty of pictures she found useful for making collages with in art lessons, and EFF mildly teased her that she liked only the pretty pastel-coloured photos, to which she responded neither with good cheer nor in a ladylike fashion; she suggested EFF might get a life, which he misheard as "wife", and retorted angrily that he was perfectly happy on his own; an unidentified voice then told Ms. Grate to E.F.F.-off, and this she promptly did so in tears, followed by a concerned RUN.

A vote was held concerning *Country Life* which required all those in favour of keeping it, to raise a hand. At first, the numbers were completely equal, and hinged on GOB, who was woken up and asked if he was in favour or not; he raised his hand, so the matter was settled, though he later mentioned that he had misheard the question as a demand by THK to "raise your hand you c**t, on your life!" which had so terrified him that he did so.

After this, MJG raised the issue of allowing pets into the CR, and reference was made in particular to dogs! DUD suggested that at least if animals (especially dogs) were clean and did not reek as if they had been bathed for weeks in their own urine, then maybe exceptions could be made, and FPS cautiously said he would look into the matter.

PIG reminded everyone present as Second Master that the Common Room's help in smoking patrols would be very much appreciated, and furthermore asked if there would be anyone willing to help him on the whole graveyard slot of the term this coming Saturday night from 10:30 to 6:30 am. TMM volunteered.

The newspaper auction was then held.

PIG then wished everyone all the best of luck with the Inspection the next day.

Minutes witnessed and signed off: RUMP & PIG

TOFFSTED INSPECTION OBSERVATION FORM

St. Cretien's College April 2010 Observed by *R.Y.*	*French* *Reginald Pompomery*

Number of pupils: *4*

Period: *6*

Lesson aims: *Looking at exam techniques, maximizing potential, etc...*

Comments: *I was interested in the way the teacher looked at specific examples of exam questions, and went through them in great detail to show how to get every point available. However, by the end of the lesson, I was surprised to find out that the practice-paper he had been going through was, in fact, the very exam that these pupils would be doing this summer.*

I enquired further, and Mr. Pompomery was very helpful indeed in showing me all the past papers and exam papers his gives to his pupils, and I can't help but notice a certain correlation between the papers he gives them to practise with and the papers he eventually gives them to do in exam weeks. There is no denying that the French department clearly gets good marks year in, year out for its pupils, averaging 85% marks; given that Mr. Pompomery actually gives the papers beforehand to all his pupils every year, I am only surprised that the pupils do not average 100% - perhaps this is an example of where a teacher should be looking at improving the performance of those less able pupils in his class...

I also notice that at actual GCSE and A-levels, the French results are always at the top of the school's own league tables; I would like to know when Mr. Pompomery has access to the papers in the days before the actual exams. Perhaps, for the sake of fairness, these should in future go through another member of his department...

TOFFSTED INSPECTION OBSERVATION FORM

St. Cretien's College April 2010 Observed by *B.A.*	*Biology* *Sonja Mangle*

Number of pupils: **16**

Period: **4**

Lesson aims: *Examining the contents of a pregnant dormouse*

Comments: *Interesting though this must have been, I'm afraid I didn't manage to stay for the whole lesson. Ms. Mangle was clear about her objectives, and I don't think her pupils were expecting anything different, but I was frankly surprised and shocked by the manner in which she opened up the mouse. For one thing, I had (perhaps naively) expected the animal to be dead, so I did find it distressing to see it squirm and wriggle as she held it down. Furthermore, I was astonished to see her attempt to cut open the mouse with a normal knife I recognised from the canteen, and which clearly did not serve its purpose, as it took several attempts and a full twelve minutes to dissect the poor creature.*

I am not altogether happy with what little I ended up seeing of this lesson; as I left, I was vaguely aware of the enthusiasm generated amongst the pupils, which suggests that Ms. Mangle is certainly an inspirational teacher, but I can't help but wonder whether she might have found a more "ordinary" or "low-key" kind of lesson to be inspected on... Suffice it to say that I ate none of the lasagne available for lunch, and I have started to think seriously about becoming a vegetarian. I must also express my worries, when I am led to believe that she intends to test how strong the human cranium is next week...

TOFFSTED INSPECTION OBSERVATION FORM

St. Cretien's College April 2010 Observed by C.N.	Games Mr. Michael Storr

Number of pupils: **34**

Period: **5**

Lesson aims: Cross country

Comments: Unbelievable. Really shocking. I watched about 150 pupils being just sent off over some of the roughest terrain in the area, and told to skirt the top of the cliff, and left to run, with their only instructions being not to come back before an hour was up.

The teacher then invited me to join him in the staff room for a coffee (which he laced generously with Cointreau, I might add), and only went outside to the terrace not to try to catch a glimpse of his pupils, but to smoke his pipe!

Never before seen such a dereliction of duty. However, on the plus side, when the pupils came back, they looked content, and admitted that this was one of their favourite lessons in the week.

Who would have guessed?...

**INSPECTION INTERIM FEEDBACK DOCUMENT
H.M. TOFFSTED INSPECTORS**

ST. CRETIEN'S COLLEGE
SEDGWICKHAM
SUSSEX

putting your pupils first

<u>IMPORTANT: THE FOLLOWING IS THE RECORD OF AN OFFICIAL DOCUMENT DRAWN UP
BY H.M. INSPECTORS FOR AND ON BEHALF OF TOFFSTED</u>

Boarding
Fine all round. It was felt by all the Inspectors that there was an excellent atmosphere for all the
pupils who board at St. Cretien's, and that plenty of activities were laid on for them at all times. The
facilities were clean and modern, and all in all we were very impressed indeed with everything we
saw. None of the pupils gave the impression of being anything less than happy at being here. Beds
and dormitories looked generally comfortable, though it was noticed that bed sheets could be
changed a little more often.

Safety and Child Protection
Really fine, and nothing much out of the ordinary to report. There had been a few incidents, we
understand, in the past, but then what school hasn't had an accident or two with all these young
children around! Overall, it was felt by all the Inspectors that the children here enjoyed a very safe
environment indeed. It was deemed that some of the irrational fears expressed by parents and
pupils were highly exaggerated.

Teaching
Absolutely fine. Fine in the extreme. Well done one and all on the teaching staff for providing the
pupils with a first-class all-round education. What we saw of the teaching, when we observed
lessons, was exemplary, and it was felt by the whole team that we had something to learn
ourselves, when we go back to our respective schools. Of particular note was how well all teaching
staff were able to integrate into their lessons a wide array of excellent best practice, and to keep
the whole experience relevant and child-centred in a thoroughly modern way.

Extra-curricular activities
Again, very fine indeed. The sheer range of sports, games and activities enthralled all of us, from
the cheese-throwing to the bog-snorkelling, from darts tournaments to all the good, regular work
that goes on down on the school farm. On any given weekend, there is a good, all-round
programme of clubs and societies for the pupils to do, and the Saturday evening disco, whilst going
on till a rather unorthodox 4.30 am, was clearly typical of a vibrant and exhilarating weekly event!
It's impressive that the whole school still makes Sunday morning Chapel at 7.00 next day, though
the Inspectors did note that there was a faint whiff of alcohol, and a number of pupils taking
Communion wine did look quite pale.

The effectiveness of governance, management and leadership
Very impressive. An altogether brilliant management structure, despite the difficulties the school
has with its overall management structure. Nonetheless, the running of the school is very smooth
indeed, and there are no complaints from either disgruntled parents or staff bristling with rage. All
in all, perfectly fine.

Compliance with regulatory requirements
Absolutely fine. There are no compliance issues at the school, and the management has ensured
that the entire site is Toffsted–compliant.

HOORAY!!

IT'S THE END OF THE

INSPECTION
PARTY !!!

Let's get down to the
Common Room Bar

this Saturday evening
7.00pm

Come on!
We deserve it!

School office memorandum – Common room notice board

Saturday Evening Detentions   17 . 4 . 10

Geoffrey Salad	single	Behaviour
Eleanor Filler	single	Smoking
Priam Hardy	single	Missing Chapel
Sally Dent	single	Smoking
George Humphrey	single	Smoking
Katie Oraface	single	Drinking
Jennifer Thwaite	single	Smoking
Priam Hardy	single	Missing period 6, Wednesday
Rebecca Balls	single	Fiddling with her lips in class
Michael Delver	single	Writing offensive rap lyrics in German lesson
Trevor Hui-Yang	double	Missing periods 3 & 4, Monday
Oscar Uncthorpe	single	Smoking in a staff garden
Frederick Sallyhope	single	Encouraging animals into unnatural behaviour
Priam Hardy	single	Defecating in a staff garden
Graham Graham	single	Establishing his own cult
Priam Hardy	single	Behaviour and inappropriate response
Vaughan Smiler	double	Loitering around staff flats
Benjamin Stroke	single	Making milk smoothies at 1 in the morning
Silas Petticoat	double	Mobile phone in Assembly
Christopher Robin	double	Fake claims of sponsorship to climb Everest
Krakker Svengus	single	Showing himself to be too full of hatred
Humboldt Bargrave	single	Showing no respect to visiting cripples

All detentions will take place in **TMM's room** (Science 9) from 7.30 pm till 10.00
Entrance to disco thereafter will be left to House Parent's discretion, case by case.

SATURDAY EVENING
STAFF DUTY PATROL REPORT

Date: 17/4/10
Duty Team Leader: Fräulein Sonja Mangle
Duty Team: PRE, DMS

Really not problems to speak of. The evening passed by without major incident. I wandered the site with my German Shepherd Blondi, and carrying a shotgun, and I enjoyed with the pupils speaking, although there were very few whom I saw.

However, I was indeed rather surprised to see the state of some of the staff this evening, who were clearly celebrating in some style the end of the Inspection week. I was very disappointed to find the kind of antics which frankly I would have disapproved of amongst our own pupils. It was my unfortunate duty to untangle the entire Art Department from out of the trees behind the Science Block, and also Blondi chanced upon Mr. D'Essise in an uncomfortable embrace with one of this year's gap students. We also dragged Thomas Horngold out from the pond.

Otherwise, though, all absolutely as quiet as a graveyard by the time I have said to my team goodbye!

SSM

Thanks, Sonja, for all the effort. I must say, it certainly was quiet this Saturday, almost eerily so! And apologies on behalf of the staff... it is true that some of them did let their hair down somewhat. Won't happen again – for another four years or so!

Peregrine

SAG

PLEASE WOULD YOU COVER THE FOLLOWING LESSON FOR: GAF

PERIOD: 2   DAY: Thurs.   DATE: 22ⁿᵈ April

MANY THANKS.

Sandra,

   Cheers for covering this Fourth Form class. They have just been introduced to Goethe's Faust, and I asked them to finish reading to the end of Part I for prep, so they should be ready to begin their essay; could you please write it on the board: "To what extent does Mephistopheles represent an alternative view of the universe, and how is this borne out within the context of this reworking of an oft-told story?" If you yourself can help advise them in any way at all, that would be really appreciated. A number of them are finding this a tough topic, and, as I am sure you know, Sturm und Drang is not always easy to grasp first time round!

Their prep is to learn the various "school subjects", the vocabulary on p. 41 of their textbooks – they will have a test on these next lesson, before ploughing on with Goethe.

Thanks again for covering them,

Gary

```
X-ViruChekked: Checked
From: Puf@stcretiens.org.uk
Date: Mon, 26 Apr 2010 10:45:02 EST
Subject: Cheryl Crauser's art work
To: Dud@stcretiens.org.uk
X-Mailer: CompuServ 2001 6.0 for Windeyes UK sub 233309
X-MD-d: Dud@school.mail
X-Return-Path: Puf@school@stcretiens.org.uk
Reply-To: Puf@school@stcretiens.org.uk
```

dud@stcretiens.org.uk

Dear Deidre,

         As Cheryl Crauser's House Mistress, I feel you should know about her recent art project. As you know, in the Third Form, we in the Art Department let the pupils explore all manner of new concepts, both in visual and material terms, and many of our Third Formers often surprise and delight us with the originality of their interpretations.

However, when Rhiannon Ninn showed me some of Cheryl's recent drawings today, I agreed with her that they seem rather troubling. She had been given the title "Flowers" which seems innocent enough, but little Cheryl's drawings tend towards something we have never seen before in the department. To say they are of a somewhat sexual nature would be a serious understatement, and the fact that (as I have heard) they are at present studying reproduction in Biology still seems unlikely to exert this sort of influence on a young mind in this way.

Might I ask you to come down and have a look at some of these drawings, as I fear she may be taking her inspiration from real life all too seriously somewhere, especially the one she called "Cross Pollination".

Much appreciated. Perhaps between the three of us we could gently persuade Cheryl to concentrate more on drawing petals and stalks with a little less imagination.

Thanks,

Petra

The St. Cretien's

Christian

Union

is meetin' next Weds

7.30pm

in the

Chapel Crypt

Subject: "**Is it US**, *or are all*

other "**religions**"

SH*T ??!!"

you gotta b there!!!

CH.cch.2477

29/04/10
45a\ref.245
CRNB

Re: Global Staff Salary Deposit Mechanisms from Feb. 2010

Dear One 'n' All!

Once again, it is that time of month when it is my painful duty to have to inform you all of a glitch in the system which allows us to pay your wages direct into your accounts. I understand how this can unsettle a number of you who have overstretched the limits of your long-term fiscal plans, and I hope you will simply find a certain solace in the way we at St. Cretien's have done the same in so spectacular a way, year on year for the last one-and-a-half centuries.

In the light of these developments, there is no alternative other than to revise the entire method of payment for the longer term. This will in due course lead to a streamlining of our outward transferral budgeting programme, and ultimately to a more comprehensive and simplified targeting of our pre-arranged co-ordinating input standards with regard to the contractual obligations of the Bursary to the so-called "teaching staff."

In the meantime, all salaries for this month will be available for picking up from the Bursary from next Thursday, between 10:45 and 10:50.

- Due to a little gremlin in the bank, salaries this month will only be available in denominations of 1p and 2p coins; staff will be able to hire security take-out bags for only £5 per pack of 20 (Used notes only please!)

- Those who arrive quickest will be more likely to be paid in the more convenient denomination of 2p; those who make our life hard by arriving at an awkward times may even find the odd ½ p and even euro coins

- Please ensure that you bring appropriate ID when collecting your salary. Drivers licences and passports are, of course, not acceptable; all staff must produce their MiDAS-approved ID documentation card. During January's "great wage giveaway" a number of members of the so-called "teaching staff" found that their salaries had been stolen, we presume by unscrupulous gremlins.

Please rest assured that we are doing all we can to improve the situation, and hope you will therefore appreciate the efforts the staff here are making.

Rtrd. Admr. Quentin Smythers BSc, FAFF, PMP, TFRREB

Bursary Doc: 223356/45a\ref.245

```
X-ViruChekked: Checked
From: Puf@stcretiens.org.uk
Date: Wed, 28 Apr 2010 16:55:43 EST
Subject: Vaughan Smiler's art work
To: Sui@stcretiens.org.uk
X-Mailer: CompuServ 2001 6.0 for Windeyes UK sub 233309
X-MD-d: Sui@school.mail
X-Return-Path: Puf@school@stcretiens.org.uk
Reply-To: Puf@school@stcretiens.org.uk
```

sui@stcretiens.org.uk

Dear Sally,
        Before contacting Vaughan Smiler's House Master about what I
am about to write, I felt it appropriate to inform you about Vaughan's
art work first. It may really be nothing, and I may just be over-
reacting, but I need to tell you about his latest art project.

As you may or may not know, Vaughan is currently in the Lower Sixth, and
is an accomplished young artist. In recent weeks, I gave the class the
title of "Through the Window" to go towards their first piece of
coursework, and was most impressed by the sequence of sketches and
paintings that Vaughan was producing.

Until, that is, one of the other pupils pointed out in front of the class
that they were in fact of you. There are a number of rather intimate
images, including several which are compromising to say the least. Each
is framed by a window, and I took the precaution of looking extensively
through the windows of your ground-floor flat in Plucker's House, and was
appalled to find that the interiors do indeed correspond with those in
the artwork.

Obviously, I need to know first and foremost whether Vaughan had your
permission or even knowledge to carry out these pieces. If he did, then
that may have to be a matter between yourselves, in which I shall promise
to remain absolutely discreet. If not, however, then I feel that Vaughan
has to answer for his actions, and at the very least apologise to you,
and hand you the offending material; if it is of any consequence, the
work is some of Vaughan's best, and if you'll allow me, the subject
matter you have provided does create a very powerful effect. Compliments!

Obviously, this needs immediate attention, as Vaughan would need as much
time as possible to catch up, if he is unable to submit these pictures,
and I would have to get him to produce some flower-filled vases sitting
on window-sills in front of landscapes as quickly as possible!

Thanks!

Petra

Dr. Anthony Ingham

<u>Memo from the Director of Studies</u>

Peregrine,

I wonder whether we ought to pop by Sc. Rm. 13 at some point on a Thursday afternoon, in order to take a look at what is going on with Sonja Mangle's activities and clubs. It cannot have escaped your notice that there is at present quite a bit of talk about what she does there, and I have had a number of pupils now complain about how dangerous some of her workshops have become. However, I am particularly concerned about a growing anti-semitic streak in the school as a whole, and it can clearly be traced to some degree back to Sonja's Thursday clubs.

Last week, Harry Dercules informed me that Sonja is in fact increasingly using any Jewish pupils present as the guinea-pigs for her more lethal trials and workshops. Apparently, last Thursday's session on industrial welding techniques was not an easy sight to experience, and I would like to try to catch her for a quick word before she undertakes next week's workshop, advertised as a practical seminar for vasectomies.

Already, some of the more scurrilous amongst my Sixth Formers are referring to her as Miss Mengele, and hypothesizing that she is the grand-daughter of the notorious Dr. Mengele who escaped to Brazil. Despite such jesting, it would be unfortunate to encourage this kind of talk by doing nothing to address the matter, and not least because the pupils are beginning to make pointed comments to her about having watched the motion picture "The Boys From Brazil." I fear she may turn on them if she realizes quite what they are insinuating.

Please can we talk further on this as soon as possible.

Anthony Ingham

Anthony Ingham, Director of Studies

From the
Examinations Officer

It is that time of year again when it is all hands on deck in order to cover all our invigilation needs. I am putting round plenty of notices, in the hope that staff don't forget their obligations at this very busy period, but the onus is very much on staff themselves to check the CR notice board as to when they are needed.

A number of points arose last summer which I should like to draw everyone's attention to again, now that the exam season is on top of us.

- Please let us have no repeat of last year's embarrassment, when the inspectors visited. They were very critical of staff bringing their own work in to exams, especially a certain lady from the Food Technology Dept. who regularly whisked cake mixture during invigilation.

- Certain members of staff last year took the rather silly game of being the first to fetch paper for pupils to the opposite extreme with particular pupils who had been troublesome for them during the year. Please remember that no matter how we may feel about the pupils in lessons, they all deserve an equal chance once they enter the Exam Hall.

- Would staff please ensure that pupils wear the correct uniform. Last year's heatwave resulted in a number of pupils allowing this rule to lapse, turning up in swimming trunks, and Robin Gallows even brought a surf board in with him. I must say I for one do not wish to see boys doing maths and the like in trunks, it just is not appropriate.

- Some teachers do take the request to move around the hall a bit too far, and the pupils did complain last year that they were quite distracted by the way in which some members of staff managed to make their way in and out of the tables at dizzying speed; I do hope that there was not any foolish competition going on among staff who are supposed to be there only for the benefit of the smooth running of the exams.

INB: MAY '10

School office memorandum – Common room notice board

<u>Saturday Evening Detentions</u>   29 . 5 . 10

Jennifer Kim	single	Being downright inscrutable
Ian Castro	double	Involving his brother in inappropriate projects
Penelope Franqueau	single	Hijacking a Spanish lesson to the detriment of all
Paul Pot	single	Refusing to learn dates for History
Simon Assad	single	Mindless aggression
Ollie Ceausescu	single	Addressing the school from the Head's balcony
Jonathan Gaddafi	single	Setting up a tent in the middle of the quad
Timothy Hitler	double	Doing a dreadful painting in Art
Freddie Amin	single	Awarding himself honours above his station
Benjamin Starline	double	Stifling artistic expression of others
Ephraim Achmeddinijad	double	Playing a dangerous game with toxic substances
Jack Mubarak	single	Being a downright unscrupulous character
Gareth Mao	double	Usurping Metalwork for his own mad ideas
Sylvia Pootine	single	Imprisoning girls in his room for singing loudly
Quentin Genghis	double	Reckless violence against others
Larry Mussolini	single	Being too punctual for his own good
Niall Mugabe	double	Running his own House into a state of ruin
Mike Hussein	double	Hiding airguns in his room (still to be located)
Zoe Milosevic	double	Hounding down pupils she felt below her
Kylie Napoleon	single	Getting too big for her boots
Tommy Caesar	single	Climbing all over Ruby Conne

All detentions will take place in **TMM's room** (Science 9) from 7.30 pm till 10.00
Entrance to disco thereafter will be left to house parent's discretion, case by case.

P255907:wrm2

31/05/10

45a\ref.117
CRNB

ST. CRETIEN'S COLLEGE
WORKS AND MAINTENANCE DEPT.

Re: H&S Directive 55902:19 (g) – Health and Safety Working Committee (HSWC)

Advance notice is hereby given regarding the implementation of H&S Directive 55902:19(g) in accordance with EU Regulations 442 & 453(h) of 1992 Commission Report pertaining to the safety of school and other institutional areas dedicated to leisure and activity-based events within the framework of organised structures, such as games and sports lessons.

It has been brought to the attention of the HSWC by recent investigation undertaken by Brian that the latent potential of serious injury or even fatalities in the St. Cretien's Swimming Pool constitutes a considerable health and safety risk. This stems mainly from the lack of sufficient barriers around the pool. What does exist is insufficient and not even fire-proof; many members of the public erroneously consider a swimming pool to be relatively free of fire risk, but should be disabused of this, as swimming pools constitute one of the most hazardous fire risks of all!

However, the most pressing issue of all is the risk of drowning, which requires immediate action at all levels. The HSWC has resolved to initiate a number of urgent committees to look into how we can reduce the risk of drowning when swimming, and hope to be able to offer some constructive proposals early next year.

Up to and until then, as a gesture to the members of staff and pupils of the school, who have insisted that the pool should remain in use, we have decided not to close the facility for the foreseeable future, so that school life can go on as normal. However, we have also decided to add sufficient salt to the water that there should be a noticeable buoyancy from now on. We have added 75 tonnes of salt and increased the temperature somewhat to assist in the process of dissolution, and Brian tested the new, safer waters yesterday, and assured me that he felt "one hundred and twelve percent safer" than before, although the local burns unit has suggested the temperature should be returned to normal. Brian will be back with us next month.

Please be sure not to imbibe any of the water, however, as this concentration of salt could result in severe sickness and vomiting.

Thank-you for your understanding in this. We hope you appreciate the importance of aiming to protect all the members of our community from the avoidable accidents that can happen.

Barry Soddum, GWTO, c/o HSWC

BS : 31/05/10

MEMORANDUM from the Second Master

DATE: 3 :06 :10

The following pupils have been suspended:

Philip Swain   Hythe House
Toby Frucker   Hythe House

- for using an air gun inappropriately.
- they will return after Leave Weekend and will sign Good Behaviour Contracts, as well as writing a full letter of apology to Olga Formost.

Baalek Solomon   Welting House
Daphne Phrasehelm   Grilling House
Pippa Deller-Jones   Cocker's House

- for engaging in lewd behaviour.
- return of all three is dependent on the release of relevant photographic evidence.

Priam Hardy   Dreer House

- for continual rudeness towards all members of staff.
- running fraudulent "business" operations within the House, selling previous years' summer exam papers to the year directly below
- for presuming academic staff will not change their summer exam material from one year to the next (and for being right, I might add, which might just wake up one or two of our Heads of Department!)
- return in two days

3. 06. 10: PIG

"A UNIQUE OPPORTUNITY" FOR ALL AGES!!!

Do you wonder how you can help to avoid to go to your dentist every year??

Fräulein MANGLE IS RUNNING AN INFORMAL

WORKSHOP for

dentistry (advanced)

ALL WELCOME, ROOM 13 BIOLOGY DEPARTM.,

SC.BUILDG   THURSDAY AT 4.P.M.

no specialist knowledge needed: OPEN WIDE!!!

snm

School office memorandum – Common room notice board

Saturday Evening Detentions   5 . 6 . 10

Simon Augustus	single	Setting himself up as someone rather special
Janice Nero	double	Continuing to play violin after fire alarm went off
Kevin Tiberius	double	Retreating into himself to the detriment of others
Julius Smith	single	Taking on our French visitors in aggressive way
Mark Antony	single	Falling in love with the wrong girl
Kyle Ligula	double	Bringing his horse into lessons
Constance Tyne	single	Being over-zealous in Chapel
David Claudius	single	Pretending to have a stammer
Billy Trajan	single	Pushing the boundaries
Gillian Querty	single	Smoking
Sadie Jingles	single	Smoking and answering back
Neil Vernon	double	Menacing juniors with voodoo curses
Lena Fluffer	single	Not knowing how to stifle yawns during Physics
Titus Stank	double	Falling in love with the wrong girl
Trevor Hui-Yang	double	Missing Friday
Val Herian	single	Allowing herself to be caught!
Frederick Sallyhope	single	Taking Farm animals back to House
Wally Hadrian	double	Building a barrier across the Lower Fields
Sally Drippe	single	Not knowing when to shut up
Priam Hardy	double	Urinating in Mr. Grueson's garden
Priam Hardy	double	Resetting several key school clocks
Priam Hardy	double	Attending an older cousin's stag-do

All detentions will take place in **TMM's room** (Science 9) from 7.30 pm till 10.00
Entrance to disco thereafter will be left to House Parent's discretion, case by case.

The Master's Lodge,
Sedgwickham,
West Sussex,

8th June, 2010

Dear Colleagues,
        I am sure you will all be saddened to hear of the sudden death of Peter Malsor, who had only three years ago retired after a staggering 38 years working at St. Cretien's in various capacities, and indeed having been an Old Cretian himself from the age of thirteen.

He arrived to teach at the school in 1961 as a Latin master, but over the years taught French, German and Spanish, helped in the Geography department and in the last seven years taught Maths to the Juniors, after having taken a correspondence degree in the subject.

Peter was also an all-round sportsman, coaching football, rugby, hockey, and of course his beloved cricket. The range and depth of his active involvement in the life of St. Cretien's is an extraordinary achievement by any standards, and the school has certainly lost one of the most committed of its Old Boys.

Furthermore, Peter was a highly popular figure in the lives of the pupils here outside their school routine, and I know he was much beloved by all the many hundreds of pupils he came into direct contact with. I am aware how his untimely death will shock many who had loved and respected Peter, especially so many of the boys for whom he remained an intimate tutor even after their time at St. Cretien's had come to an end.

Peter never married, and had no family to speak of, and in his will he has left a considerable and very generous amount of money to the school to which he dedicated most of his life. However, quite unusually, he has also made a most unorthodox request, given his attachment to the place, and this is that his coffin might be allowed to stand for a while in Grand Hall, where he spent so much time as man and boy.

I have decided to allow this, and I hope you will not find the presence of Peter's coffin on its catafalque in the middle of Grand Hall in any way disturbing. It was decided by the governors and myself that Peter's original request for the lid to be left off and for a single red rose to be placed in his mouth would have been inappropriate in a place where children as young as thirteen are rushing between lessons, so the lid will remain on.

Peter's wake will last for four weeks. I trust you will emphasise to the children that they should show due respect when they pass, and that any graffiti or attempts to open the coffin will will be treated as a serious disciplinary offence.

Yours faithfully,

A. K. Warble

ALAN WARBLE, BA CANTAB, Dip Ed

The Master's Lodge,
Sedgwickham,
West Sussex,

15th June, 2010

Dear Mr. & Mrs Synide,
        Thank-you for for your letter of the 7th June, outlining your concerns about your son Gerard. I understand your worries that he is in danger of failing yet again in his core subjects at GCSE, and I also understand that he has shown willing in trying now for a number of years to resit the exams, in the hope of obtaining some of the essential qualifications he will need in the wider world outside.

However, despite the fact that year on year you have continued to pay the full fees in line with inflation, and although I understand that these fees have indeed contributed very much to St. Cretien's over Gerard's time here, the management agree with me that it is probably time for him to face leaving the school, and to see how he fares amongst people of his own age.

Not only is it felt to be a little inappropriate, now that Gerard has reached his thirtieth birthday, for him to be in classes with children, some as young as fifteen, but I do sense that the moment has finally arrived for him to take some responsibility in the direction he is taking. I have to say that I do not agree at all with your comments that the school should in some way burden any guilt with regard to your son's lack of progress over the last fifteen years, nor that any of our teachers feel any attachment to his being in their lessons. In fact many teachers have come and gone in the meantime, and some of those teaching him at present were barely born when he first arrived at St. Cretien's.

I hope Gerard soon finds his place in the world, and that he enjoys the thrill of exploring life beyond the cloisters of St. Cretien's. Thank-you all for your much-appreciated support of the school over these years, and I shall not be alone in saying that Gerard's familiar, shuffling figure will be sorely missed by us all next September.

Yours sincerely,

Q. K. Warble

ALAN WARBLE, BA CANTAB, Dip Ed

MEMORANDUM from the Second Master

DATE: 13 :06 :10   **RE:**   Peter Malsor's Coffin

Please would all staff remain vigilant around Peter Malsor's coffin in Grand School. There has recently been a spate of pupils placing various objects on top, from a framed photograph of Elvis to a pair of girl's knickers and bra, and on Wednesday even a plastic beaker filled with someone's urine. I have already authorised a police check on this for any trace of alcohol or other illegal substance.

Of course, you will be aware that the most serious of all was last night, and in fact we should all, not just Peter's memory, feel violated in some way by the removal of his coffin from its stand, and by the sight of it propped up on its end in front of the blackboard in Geoffrey Bernay's classroom.

Things are not helped by the fact that Geoffrey, going in especially early this morning to prepare his lessons, fainted and was only found by Mrs. Huang King, of the cleaning staff at 7.30. However, I have been on the telephone to the hospital, and they have assured me that Geoffrey will be back home this evening.

The maintenance staff have since place Peter back on his pedestal, and assured me that he is still well lodged inside. Please remain alert with regard to this, and do report any strange noises to Security. Barry and Brian are looking into making the catafalque more secure.

Peregrine I. Grueson

13/06/10: PIG

We think we may have reached a turning
point. The chap in charge here seems to have
been ousted by someone else (I almost wrote
"outed", but I suspect none of these fellows
is a closet transvestite!!!). Anyway, this
new chap appears quite keen to get rid
of us, and has told us that tomorrow we
are to be taken down into the jungle to
meet up with some negotiators, and set
free; they're also going to lay on rooms
with hot running water, a buffet and
some entertainment + live music. It sounds
too good to be true, but the children (who've behaved
impeccably all this time) are getting quite restless, and are
looking forward to getting away from here. See you soon! **Tim**

The Common Room,
St. Cretien's Coll.,
Sedgwickham,
West Sussex,
Inghiliterra.

Hello there everybody! How are things?
Can't believe it's been almost a year since
we've been away... some of the pupils are
worried that they'll have to redo the Fifth
Form when they get back, and they're
not v happy! Honestly, that's the least of
our worries! Last week, we were driven
out to a huge plantation of some sort and
forced to pick the strangest crop I've ever
seen. Poor Paula Simbiotica tried some
and she still hasn't come round. Anyway,
we seem to be free of any executions here,
and the five pupils who have lost fingers
have been jolly decent about it all. Hope to speak to you all
very soon, as soon as we get transferred to a place with a phone ! **Tim**

The Common Room,
St. Cretien's Coll.,
Sedgwickham,
West Sussex,
Inglaterra.

Statue of
St. Cretien

School office memorandum – Common room notice board

<u>Saturday Evening Detentions</u>   25 . 6 . 11

Sally Dunkster	double	Entering Frl. Mangle's lab before being asked
Petula Hayley	single	Being 30 seconds late for Frl. Mangle
Terence Rollio	double	Being two minutes late for Frl. Mangle
Gareth Hulk	single	Not understanding Frl. Mangle's accent
Fiona Jellifer	single	Not saying "Guten Tag, Frl. Mangle"
Xavier Balls	double	Using wrong colour in Frl. Mangle's prep
Henry Powte	single	Saying "my father teaches here" to Frl. Mangle
Sonja Verrily	single	Getting Frl. Mangle annoyed by sighing
Benjamin Torque	double	Looking out of Frl. Mangle's lab window
Devlin Fukulver	single	Doing wrong exercise for Frl. Mangle
William Jellbose	single	Not underlining title in Frl. Mangle's prep
Celine Prendle	double	Fidgeting while Frl. Mangle talked
Harry Thomas	single	Turning round in Frl. Mangle's lesson
Sunjiit Panjavi	single	Misunderstanding Frl. Mangle's humour
Serena Goaf	double	Not hearing Frl. Mangle
Pauline Ratthold	double	Wrong answer in Frl. Mangle's class
Kelly Maisy	single	Arguing back in Frl. Mangle's class
Priam Hardy	single	Spitting and swearing at Frl. Mangle
Silo Silover	single	Refusing to listen to Frl. Mangle
Duncan McDuncan	double	Crying when being talked to by Frl. Mangle
Geruthra Geriolia-Smith	single	Watching Frl. Mangle walking in the Cloisters
Brian Brain	single	Putting out deckchairs in Frl. Mangle's classroom

All detentions will take place in **TMM's room** (Science 9) from 7.30 pm till 10.00
Entrance to disco thereafter will be left to House Parent's discretion, **case by case.**

TO THE VISITING PUBIC USING THESE FACILITIES:

<u>PLEASE NOTE</u>

<u>VERY HOT WATER</u> INDEED

PLEASE DO NOT TURN THIS TAP OF TO MUCH, AS THIS WILL DAMAGE IT <u>BEYOND REPAIR</u>.

A NUMBER OF COLLEAGUE'S HAVE ALL READY SCOLDED THEMSELVE'S WITH THIS WATER, AND HAVE THEN STRUCK THE TAP IN A FIT OF PEAK. THIS WILL DAMAGE THE TAP TOO, AND SHOULD BE AVOIDED.

IF IN ANY DOUBT AT ALL, USE THE COLD TAP, BUT BE AWARE THAT THIS TAP DRIP'S FOR A LONG TIME AFTER TURNING OFF, SO PLEASE DO NOT TURN IT OFF TOO MUCH.

THANK-YOU

ENJOY WHEREVER YOU ARE GOING TO, AND PLEASE TELL US IF YOU BELIEVE THESE FACILITIE'S ARE FAULTY

ST. CRETIEN'S COLLEGE,
WEST SUSSEX,

FROM THE SECOND MASTER

Second Master's Lodge,
22nd June, 2010

Re: Rehearsals for Summer Concert

Dear Trevor,

      I would like to begin by thanking you for all the work you're putting into the preparations for this weekend's Summer Concert. I am sure it is going to be a great success, as is always the case with this event put on by your department. Both the Head Master and myself are fully aware of the sheer amount of time you devote to your work, and in particular for just such major events as this coming concert, and we appreciate what you have achieved in raising the Music Department's profile so much in the five years you have been at St. Cretien's. We both understand how much these concerts promote the school to the wider public, and we are sympathetic to the work that goes into them on all sides.

However, we are becoming very worried about reports coming in from colleagues concerned with just how much time the children are sacrificing to this concert, and though we all know that they are often wont to, shall we say, find any excuse for postponing their prep, it would be fair to say that expecting all the players to be present at rehearsals five nights a week from 6.30 till 10.00 is liable to be placing too much pressure on some of our pupils. I am thinking here not just of our juniors, who are apt to become very tired if they are too late to bed, but it is also rather too much for our pupils doing their GCSEs and A-levels. This morning, Damien Drew overslept through most of his economics exam, citing a choir rehearsal with you last night which went on until they had perfected a particular warm-up exercise, apparently until 10.45…

A programme beginning with Brahms' German Requiem and Stravinsky's Rite of Spring in the first half, followed by Mahler's Sixth Symphony might prove to have been a little too ambitious in the event, and perhaps will force us to scrutinise the content of our concerts in time for next year's Christmas and Summer Concerts.

I hope this timely reminder does not in any way dampen your enthusiasm on the eve of your big night, but perhaps in future we might discuss beforehand what would be an appropriate programme. Many thanks again for all your efforts.

Yours sincerely,

Peregrine I. Grueson

Fourth Form

SUMMER TERM BIOLOGY EXAM

Time allowed: 1hour 30 mins

Answer at least TWO of the following questions

1. Discuss how Scientologists find a way of explaining the complexity and innate beauty of a bird's wing.

2. What could prove the existence of Thetans in a universe dominated by the material study of life merely in terms of cells and chemical reactions?

3. Explain in terms of traditional Scientologist theories the way in which Darwinism is the biological equivalent of a large, steaming pile of bovine excrement.

4. How is the modern study of Biology consistent with the lifestyle that regular Auditing through the teachings of our Founder L. Ron Hubbard can help us all to achieve?

5. Describe the workings of the human digestive system, with especial reference to the <u>duodenum</u>

Please ensure that your set teacher's initials are written clearly at the top of each new sheet you use.

S.M.F. – 21/6/10

23/6/10<ASI

<u>**To:**</u> *Reginald Pompomery*

Reginald,

       Regarding the attached Third Form French exam which was set last Tuesday; having looked at it for a while since it has been in general circulation, I can't help but feel that it is a little simplistic, even for some of our less gifted pupils.

Given that it has since transpired that this is the selfsame exam that has been used since 1997, I wonder whether it might now be time for a new exam in this slot? I appreciate your attempt to widen the pupils' general, cultural knowledge, but I am sure this could take the form of a slightly more taxing test.

Thank-you very much!

Anthony Ingham

Anthony Ingham, Director of Studies

LA FRANCE ET LES FRANÇAIS
<u>Combien sais-tu?</u>

A general knowledge quiz for the Third Form!

<u>Total time: 1hr</u>

1. Combien d'habitants y a-t-il en France?
    - a). 40
    - b). 41
    - c). 401
    - d). 60 000 000

2. Comment s'appelle la capitale de la France?
    - a). Paris
    - b). Le Mississippi
    - c). Charles Dickens
    - d). Chris Tarrant

3. Qui est le Président de la France?
    - a). President Bush
    - b). President Camembert
    - c). Elvis Presley
    - d). Nicolas Sarkozy

4. Lequel est une montagne?
    - a). une table
    - b). un cahier
    - c). un, deux, trois
    - d). Mont Blanc

5. Quelle est la langue officielle de la France?
    - a). le français
    - b). l'italien
    - c). Languedoc
    - d). longtemps

6. Laquelle est une spécialité de la France?
    - a). βλαμανχισ
    - b). тандорй коррй
    - c). خ ث ضك ضدﻱ ﺆﺋل
    - d). le vin

7. Laquelle est une ville française?
    - a). Toulouse
    - b). Timbouctou
    - c). Kentucky
    - d). Scotland

8. Qui était un héros français?
    - a). L'Oncle Sam
    - b). Macbeth
    - c). Mac the Knife
    - d). Gen. de Gaulle

9. L'axe franco-allemand consiste en:
    a). Le Japon et la Belgique
    b). L'Iran et l'Irak
    c). L'Angleterre et l'Écosse
    d). La France et l'Allemagne

10. Lequel était un roi français?
    a). Prince Albert
    b). Robert Mugabe
    c). Tyrannosaurus Rex
    d). Louis XIV

11. Quel animal est le symbole de la France ?
    a). le zèbre
    b). l'éléphant
    c). le cobra
    d). le coq français

12. Quel dialecte est un dialecte français?
    a). Welsh
    b). le Geordie
    c). Received Pronunciation
    d). le Provençal

13. Comment s'appelle l'hymne national français ?
    a). Dieu Sauvez la Reine
    b). Star Spangled Banner
    c). Thriller
    d). la Marseillaise

14. Lequel est un fromage français ?
    a). Double Gloucester
    b). Danish Blue
    c). Tesco's-own Processed
    d). La Vache Qui Rit

15. La France a reçu son nom de quelle tribu ?
    a). les Zulus
    b). les Inuits (Esquimeaux)
    c). Mongolian Nomads
    d). les Francs

16. Quelle marque de voiture provient de France ?
    a). Lada
    b). Mitsubishi
    c). Mercedes-Benz
    d). Citroën

Be sure to answer all the questions, and if you are not sure of the correct answer, remember it could still be worth making a lucky guess !

RHP

School office memorandum – Common room notice board

Saturday Evening Detentions   26 . 6 . 10

Joseph Green	single	Ruining Macbeth for everyone else
John Brooke	single	Fathering twenty children without permission
Gustave Painter	single	Going on and on
Arnie Finemount	single	Singing in a silly voice
Dick Ostrich	single	Being a Don Juan around school
Tony Bridger	single	Unfinished work
Chris Merry	single	Taking his teacher to hell and back
Anthony Weaver	single	Serial crimes
Alban Mount	single	Putting ear to the ground to disrupt lessons
Dick Risker	single	Stealing other people's jewellery
John-Philip Bough	single	Coming late to the junior opera
Priam Hardy	double	Trying to argue his way out of a bad situation
Deborah Ussi	single	Never getting anything really resolved
Frank Shoebert	single	Not finishing his last piece of coursework
Robert Shoebloke	single	Being ridiculously obsessive about his girlfriend
Jake Littlered	single	Thieving like a magpie
George Trade	double	Having a fireworks party with loud music
Lenny Amberstone	single	Glossing over a serious school feud in song
Jonny Cage	single	Unofficial sponsored silence
Freddie Circler	single	Fiddling too much
Frederick Chopin	single	Taking his studies too seriously
Maximillian Breech	single	Fantasizing about Scotland

All detentions will take place in **TMM's room** (Science 9) from 7.30 pm till 10.00
Entrance to disco thereafter will be left to House Parent's discretion, case by case.

THE ST. CRETIEN'S

DEBATING SOCIETY

Please join us in the Library for this week's debate,
followed by tea, coffee and biscuits

This week's motion:

THIS HOUSE BELIEVES THAT COLOURED FOLK HAVE A MORAL ADVANTAGE

*

Thursday, 7.30 pm

Please ensure you obtain your Housemaster's / Housemistress'
permission beforehand

P255778:wrm2

29/06/10

45a\ref.145
CRNB

ST. CRETIEN'S COLLEGE
WORKS AND MAINTENANCE DEPT.

Re: H&S Directive 42110:6 (c) – Health and Safety Working Committee (HSWC)

Advance notice is hereby given regarding the implementation of H&S Directive 42110:6 (c) pertaining to the use or otherwise of the mobile crane (extendable single-armed cherrypicker). This follows a serious accident this week in which Barry found himself hospitalised for a number of days.

In our admirable attempts here at the HSWC to test a number of everyday situations in order to establish the extent to which they constitute a threat to public safety, we recently felt resolved to understand how far the arm of the crane could be raised while fully loaded with Barry.

As a number of staff who had gathered in the Quad were able to witness, we were completely successful in establishing how far the crane could lean, though the insensitive reaction of the spectators was not helpful in extracting Barry from the wreckage, and their names have been noted.

May we take this opportunity to remind you all that we here at the HSWC exist only to ensure the smooth running of our lives here, and we take our role here very seriously indeed. Do please feel free to sign the card on the Common Room mantelpiece for Barry, unless you are one of the members of staff who did nothing to help him on the day.

Hoping you have another safe day here on the school site – it doesn't happen by chance.

Brian Blouse, GWTO, c/o HSWC

BB : 29/06/10

The St. Cretien's
Christian Union
is meetin' next Tues

7.30pm

in the

Chapel Crypt

Yo! Yo!

Subject: "Is God a CLASS A

drug, coz HE make us

high man!!!"

kerpow!!

School office memorandum – Common room notice board

Saturday Evening Detentions　　3 . 7 . 10

Priam Hardy	single	Poor response to being on red card
Priam Hardy	single	Mindless aggression in Ed. for Living
Priam Hardy	single	Snorting illegal substances
Priam Hardy	single	Being out of House at 4.30 am
Priam Hardy	single	Setting fire to Mr. Grueson's car
Priam Hardy	double	Smoking

All detentions will take place in **TMM's room** (Science 9) from 7.30 pm till 10.00

Entrance to disco thereafter will be left to House Parent's discretion, case by case.

SCHOOL OFFICE : 3.7.10

SATURDAY EVENING
STAFF DUTY PATROL REPORT

Date: 3/7/10
Duty Team Leader: Peregrine Grueson
Duty Team: TMM, SER

What an extraordinary evening! I am forever amazed and fascinated by the boundless energy of our pupils, and delighted by their originality and wit. As ever, one would always expect at this very late stage of the year a certain degree of excitement. And this year was no exception, but we cannot become too agitated and mean-spirited about the way the boys and girls let off their end-of-year steam!

Early on in the evening, I counted only a dozen or so cases of blatant drunkenness, and confiscated only about half a dozen empty vodka bottles, so all in all, pretty quiet at this stage.

With the beginning of tonight's "Anarchy Punk" themed disco, a number of incidents occurred involving the outbreak of fights, including a couple of hot-spots where knives were in evidence. I successfully persuaded the groups to break up, and managed to secure some solemn promises indeed from those with the largest blades. I confiscated a so-called "knuckle-duster" but unfortunately this had been pickpocketed from my jacket before the evening was out.

On the whole, it was not too bad an evening, even after Priam Hardy was released from his mega detention session, and after the fire brigade had put out the small incidents in the car park and then moved on to extinguishing all the bins on the site, we were finally able to deal with the police who had turned up in response to a (rather miserable) phone call from a member of the public about the rave that had moved on to the centre of Sedgwickham.

My team and I cleaned up round the barricades after official lock-up at 2.am, and then we did patrols around the backs of all the buildings and around the site. Many thanks indeed to Timothy Munt, who was very much my right hand man tonight, and who then happily continued on through the night until dawn.

Altogether a most successful night, certainly in comparison with previous years. Thanks to all involved !

Peregrine

X-ViruChekked: Checked
From: Hip@stcretiens.org.uk
Date: Sun, 4 Jul 2010 16:44:56 EST
Subject: Summer Concert
To: elliehopes@s-herald.org.uk
X-Mailer: CompuServ 2001 6.0 for Windeyes UK sub 233309
X-MD-d: elliehopes@s-herald.org.uk
X-Return-Path: hip@school@stcretiens.org.uk
Reply-To: hip@school@stcretiens.org.uk

elliehopes@s-herald.org.uk

Dear Ellie,

An epic concert of unheard-of length ended up being a tragedy of epic
proportions too. It is almost too good to be believed; you really had to
be there. I was, because I had been reliably informed down at the Hare
and Hounds that they are always worth going to for sheer comedic value.
Def worth sacrificing a Sat night for! Next year you need to be here to
write a piece about it all, honestly!

It was to have begun at 6.30, given that it was already envisaged to last
a good 3 and a half hours. But no-one could find either the lead violin
or Trevor the Head of Music who was to conduct it. It turns out that
Trevor had had an attack of nerves and invited his lead violinist for a
pre-show settler or two, but what had started out as a tot of Dutch
courage left them both much the worse for wear and totally oblivious to
the time.

They then spilled onto the stage in Grand School (still adorned by the
now definitely swelling Peter Malsor) past all the parents in an
absolutely blind panic, mumbling their apologies, bumping into chairs,
kicking handbags and still struggling with their bow-ties! The concert
eventually started at 7.10.

Anyway I learned later that the lead violinist had been telling Trevor
about the pupil's big fear being speed, as they simply felt
underprepared, despite having done no French or German prep for me for 4
and a half weeks. So despite the late start, the two of them had agreed
to slow the whole thing down.

And with drunken thoroughness they very nearly brought Brahms' German
Requiem to an utter standstill! A piece which normally lasts an hour and
a quarter was drawn out over a spellbinding two hours, with a couple of
the slower moments so heavy and lugubrious that the whole atmosphere
around the shiny black coffin hung dripping with morbid depression.

The Rite of Spring didn't do much to alter things either, with all its
normally pounding rhythms hammered out so relentlessly slowly that the
audience was by now almost drummed into awful, hypnotic submission. So
the interval came as some relief at last with wine, vol-au-vents, canapes
etc..

But worse was yet to come. The conductor and his lead fiddler needed more Dutch courage for their fraying nerves, and so all remaining vestiges of coherence now disappeared, in indirect proportion to their determination to get things right and to please.

They had clearly decided that things had indeed gone too slowly in the first half, so they now resolved to speed things up a bit for Mahler's Sixth. Stumbling onto his podium at 9.30, Trev tapped his baton and started the orchestra off a such a pace that nobody could really keep up, least of all the audience. The lead violin was way too drunk to follow his own score, let alone try to set a pace for the pupils around him, and even the slow movement raced along so fast that the mysterious cowbells sounded more like the rattling bells on a steamtrain thundering through the Alps.. By the time they reached the huge finale, the whole orchestra was worn out and unsure of where they were, and the entire audience in Grand School was sitting through a vast wall of noise which made no sense to anyone. It was truly priceless! The music collapsed and disintegrated around the twisted faces of the pupils, and the final few seconds were so shocking for all the wrong reasons that a number of parents had their hands over their ears.

Exhausted by the whole fiasco, and not wanting to deal with the thin applause from the much diminished audience, Trevor rushed to make his getaway, stumbled drunkenly off the podium and missed the stage steps. He careered down the middle of the spectators, and headed straight towards the coffin, crashing headlong into it and toppling it off its catafalque, from where it fell towards the nearby parents, bursting open and allowing Peter's bloated corpse to bounce out like a grinning jack-in-the-box, before sliding over the polished floor! Much hysterical screaming, shouting, jumping around, pupils and parents alike jumping into each others' arms! Much vomiting..

The Head quietly promised refunds.

I am already looking forward to the next big extravaganza by the Music Dept. They'll have some trouble topping last night!

Can't wait to see you after your stint in Scotland,

Love xx

Henry

The Master's Lodge,
Sedgwickham,
West Sussex,

4th July, 2010

Dear Trevor,

Please come to have a word with me about last night's Summer Concert tomorrow lunchtime. I see you are free on Period 6 on Mondays, so perhaps that would be a good time to pop into the Lodge.

Thank-you and see you then.

Yours,

A. K. Warble

ALAN WARBLE, BA CANTAB, Dip Ed

Mr. Trevor King – Director of Music

COMMON ROOM NOTICE BOARD

Please note some of the typographical errors I have managed to pick up in this term's batch of reports. I can only repeat and emphasise, as every year, how important it is for us at St. Cretien's to give at least an outward impression of professionalism and care, and such mistakes as these only serve to undermine the good reputation we so need in this all-too competitive market.

Please therefore be vigilant with your typing, and be aware of the following common errors which seem to have bypassed the spell-check, or which were accidentally "auto-corrected" by the computer itself. Thank-you.

torn	not	*porn*
flagged up	not	*shagged up*
Tito	not	*tiptoes*
coped	not	*copulated*
triggering	not	*frigging*
climatic	not	*climactic*
buns	not	*bums*
butter up	not	*buttocks up*
public	not	*pubic*
Tito	not	*tits*
priority	not	*priapic*
crutch	not	*crotch*
flagging behind	not	*a sagging behind*
taking umbrage	not	*taken up the bridge*
sodden eyes	not	*sodomize*
penitential	not	*pent-up testicle*
straining	not	*staining*
humbug	not	*humped up*
spin back	not	*sperm bank*
spam diner	not	*sperm donor*

Thank-you for your vigilance.

Anthony Ingham

Anthony Ingham, Director of Studies

P255677:wrm2

05/07/10

45a\ref.114
CRNB

ST. CRETIEN'S COLLEGE
WORKS AND MAINTENANCE DEPT.

Re: H&S Directive 42079:12 (b) – Health and Safety Working Committee (HSWC)

Advance notice is hereby given regarding the implementation of H&S Directive 42079:12 (b) in accordance with EU Regulations 497 & 498(a) of 1992 Commission Report and File 112, pertaining to external fire-doors in workspaces combining multiple routes or means of traffic, human or otherwise.

It has been brought to the attention of the HSWC by recent investigation undertaken on behalf of the County Council Health and Safety Executive (Fire Department) that there is an urgent need of fire-proof doors in both lateral arcades of the Main Quad Cloister. It has therefore been decided that a series of heavy-duty, double-hinged swinging fire-doors will be fitted at regular intervals in both lateral arcades, conforming to European standards, as detailed in the Commission Report mentioned above, as well as facilitating easy access to all areas of the Main Quad. Given the sensitivity of the site, as well as the need for us to consult with members of the teaching staff who use the site on an everyday basis, we hope that this advance notice will allow all users of the Main Quad not to be unduly worried or surprised when the doors are installed over the weekend.

With safety uppermost on the Working Committee's agenda, it has also been decided to take this opportunity to address a number of other issues with regard to the Main Quad.

a). With recent slips and falls due to the inclement weather at a record high, it is recommended that the arterial routes around and across the Main Quad should be resurfaced with immediate effect from this weekend; in consultation with ground staff, we have opted for a non-slip, rubber-based "playground-style" flexible matting, which will allow us to conform to the EU safety regulations and compliance guidelines. It will of course also be fire- and trip-proof.

b). In order to prevent pupils and staff from endangering their lives by cutting across wet lawns, a high-security fence is to be constructed around all the lawn-zones, whose fine mesh should still allow unspoilt views of the major features of the Quad to be enjoyed. It is intended to top this with barbed wire and the type of CCTV cameras which have already proved so useful in monitoring the staff in Common Room.

c). The Fountain, an area where there is an ever-present danger of drowning, is to be replaced with a waterless work by local Sedgwickham artist Trevor Bile, responsible for the successful Shinball Memorial Fountain.

d). A pedestrian crossing will be installed under the West Arch. Given the number of reckless drivers exceeding the new Quad Area speed-limit of 0.5mph, this is regarded as extremely urgent. A part-time position of Crossing Warden will be established in order to ensure that this zone works effectively during peak hours.

Helping the world to help itself and for itself,

Brian Blouse, GWTO, c/o HSWC

BB : 05/07/10

FROM THE
HEAD OF MUSIC
St. Cretien's College
TREVOR KING

DATE: 7/7/10   **RE:**   Raising St. Cretien's profile

Peregrine,

I am writing to test out an idea with you, before going on to suggest it to the Head Master. I am not sure whether you are aware or not, but the Head did express a few doubts he had with me about this year's Summer Concert, and I am quite keen to put the Music Department back on a surer footing with him. So please do tell me your thoughts about this as an idea.

It occurred to me while I was wandering through my department last night, turning off lights, when I accidentally chanced upon a number of our colleagues rehearsing for next week's staff party. I think you know who I mean: the same five old rockers who get together rather embarrassingly every week in the school Rehearsal Hall, using the department's drum kit and setting up their amplifiers as if they are on tour! I can't help but feel sorry for them, as they clearly feel they once had a chance of playing with the big boys, as it were, yet it is painfully obvious that these weekly "sessions" are just a way of dealing with their various mid-life crises, if you ask me.

The fact that they often attract a huddle of curious pupils presumably flatters their egos quite a bit, though these pupils seem merely curious and frankly embarrassed at seeing their French/Chemistry/Physics/English teachers rocking around, getting static feedback and "wah-wah" effects, whilst running through a number of jaw-achingly awful 80's rock anthems. The drummer is particularly hilarious, with his inability to keep any semblance of rhythm or do anything more interesting than bang away looking earnestly savage! If I hear their version again of "We Will Rock You" I reckon it might make me think again about coming to the end-of-year staff party, where we're all supposed to frolic madly to their "entertainment."

Anyway, it got me wondering whether perhaps we could invite a real rock star/group into the school next year, as a way of boosting the school's public profile. I still have a number of friends in the entertainment business, and might just be able to pull a few strings or more with some people in the TV industry. What do you think about linking up with a production team for some kind of reality TV programme, in which a true legend comes to the school to give lessons on being a rock star?

Do let me know whether you think this might be something I could run past the Head, once he is talking to me again.

Yours,

Trevor King

Welting House

8th July, 2010

The Head Master,
St. Cretien's School,
West Sussex

Dear Mr. Warble,

This is just a quick note to let you know how my Youth Enterprise Club is going, now that we have had a couple of terms to let it settle down.

I should begin by saying that, after an initial few weeks of membership in just single figures, by the time we reached Easter, we were up to over twenty pupils, turning up each week, and putting some serious time and energy into their group projects. I have to admit, I am delighted with the way the activity has taken off, and how genuinely enthusiastic all the participants are. We have some of the brightest pupils taking part, and some of them are finding that their ideas are proving very interesting indeed.

At present, we are tentatively exploring how the markets are reacting to the current woes out there, and one or two of my group are clearly making headway against the tide!

Thanks again for your support in this.

Yours,

Henry Pukeman

ST. CRETIEN'S COLLEGE
ACCOUNTS DEPARTMENT

The Bursary, Churchill House, School Lane

7	No. 59927	RE:B9	ibbn/y/98 Eamon Fuller / teaching staff	TOTAL
87	775644 – ttu			
			sundry expenses overdue on phone bill	£0.21

FINAL DEMAND

please remit immediately!!

Please settle asap! Thank-you   £0.21p

CH.cch.2477

8/07/10
45a\ref.278
CRNB

Re: Outstanding debts amongst staff, tax year 2009-2010

Dear One 'n' All!

A quite serious point about unpaid bills. As you are probably already aware, thanks to a number of gremlins in the way we present news from Accounts, things on this side of the court are not at all rosy at the moment. However, that could be remedied at a single stroke, as our own accountants have explained.

A good number of staff do have a certain amount of money outstanding against their name, due mainly to occasional bills that have not been totally wrapped up. Some of these bills may seem paltry to those individuals involved, but combined with the accrued interest and diaphoretic distortion of monetary calibration, the Accounts Department have calculated that the whole differential in the shortfall from such sundry unpaid bills amounts to an incredible £4.5m.

Needless to say, this kind of sum would solve St. Cretien's financial problems literally within seconds, and therefore, please could staff see their way to settling these bills at once. We are, as ever, fully at your service here in the Bursary Department, so do form an orderly queue, why don't you!!

Thank-you for your prompt response.

Rtrd. Admr. Quentin Smythers BSc, FAFF, PMP, TFRREB

Bursary Doc: 2234452/45a\ref.278

8/7/10<ASI

<u>COMMON ROOM NOTICE BOARD</u>

This is an important memo for **ALL** members of teaching and pastoral staff, regarding the **PERSONAL** "e"-mail I sent yesterday to Peregrine Grueson.

Please ignore it completely, and if possible erase it from your memories.

On no account talk about it to other staff, and **ABSOLUTELY DO NOT TALK TO THE PUPILS ABOUT IT.**

Being still quite new to the whole "e"-mailing thing and all that, I did accidentally press on the "send to all" button on the screen, and I am afraid that the content of my note to Peregrine was there for all to see. However, if you have not yet opened it up, please would you be so kind as to refrain from doing so.

Needless to say, what I mentioned in the "e"-mail is not for public consumption, and is merely my private reflections on where the Head Master might be in the trajectory of his long and illustrious career. There is not a jot or scintilla of hard evidence that he will be retiring next year, nor indeed has he spoken about this to myself or to anyone else. So please do not presume that I know anything that others do not know; and rest assured that, if I did, then the staff would, of course, be among the first to know.

So please ignore anything you have read, heard or presumed. And in future, please conduct any correspondence with me on paper or in person; I shall not in future be using "e"-mail.

Anthony Ingham

Anthony Ingham, Director of Studies

Greetings all! Good news about Paula, who
has made a full recovery after being comatose
for an amazing three weeks! We are all so
proud of her, though she has no idea who
we are or where she is. Still, we're grateful
for small mercies! Hope your Summer
Term has started well. We are actually
hopeful of being back before Half Term
because, the group holding us has just
changed its revolutionary constitution,
and doesn't believe in hostages any more.
Don't know how they plan to get rid of us
out here in the middle of nowhere, but I
guess they'll drive us to the nearest airfield
and book us flights back home. Fingers crossed!! Bye! Tim

The Common Room,
St. Cretien's Coll.,
Sedgwickham,
West Sussex,
Inglaterra.

X-ViruChekked: Checked
From: Hip@stcretiens.org.uk
Date: Fri, 2 Jul 2010 12:56:12 EST
Subject: Girl with visions!!
To: elliehopes@s-herald.org.uk
X-Mailer: CompuServ 2001 6.0 for Windeyes UK sub 233309
X-MD-d: elliehopes@s-herald.org.uk
X-Return-Path: hip@school@stcretiens.org.uk
Reply-To: hip@school@stcretiens.org.uk

elliehopes@s-herald.org.uk

Dear Ellie,

Here's a weird one which I only got to hear about a few days ago. She's
called Sally Delver, and suffice to say that she has spent the year
convincing herself that she could see devils, receive holy visions and
speak to the Good Lord Himself, no less.

I reckon she'll calm down once she goes home and has all the summer to
cool off a bit, so I don't think you'll have much of a story, come
September. But she is an interesting case. She used to appear on
detention lists for smoking, etc, but now it's more likely to be because
she's seen Saint Peter in front of her, unlocking her bedroom with his
heavenly bunch of keys, or just happened to scream out the Lord's Prayer
in the middle of hockey! Some of the other girls think it's funny, but a
growing number of them in her boarding house have begun to believe that
she is bringing them victory in the House Leagues, and a small cult seems
to have developed around her. Needless to say, she is always the first to
be chosen for a team in games lessons, and she is even considered a must
to have on your coach when there are any school trips. She gives out
advice on chastity and sex, and also deals fearlessly with the giant
spiders infesting the rafters of the boarding houses, earning her the
title "The Arachni-saint". Bullied juniors petition her to intervene, and
the bullies themselves come to her for confession!

Obviously, the Chapel has done everything it can to put a cap on this,
though apparently without much success. Apparently, she has called for
the whole Chapel to be excommunicated because it isn't catholic and
dynamic enough. The Chapel responded this weekend by having a preacher
come who gave a sermon on the subject of false prophets, during which the
girl threw up, and then claimed to see the face of an angry Jesus in her
vomit. The other kids loved it.

I hope you're glad with the scoop I got you regarding next year's
rebranding event! Not only that, but rumours are now rife that the Head
will almost definitely be leaving next summer, so there's already a great
deal of secretive discussion as to what his legacy should be. Apparently,
before he goes, he wants to make sure he is remembered by some grand and
noteworthy addition to the school! Plus, I hear there's even a real
possibility that we might even be getting involved with a TV reality
programme too... Whatever next?!

Love xx

Henry

MEMORANDUM from the Second Master

DATE: 9:07:10   **RE:** HM Speech

Once again, this is a plea to all staff to attend the Head Master's speech at the end of the term. Earlier in the school year, there seemed to be something of an improvement, but numbers have once again fallen off, and it is most unsettling for just a few of us to be up there on the stage (thanks TMM). Furthermore, when there are a good many of us up there, it is much less noticeable to the pupils if something goes wrong. Only three weeks ago, you may have heard that GOB fell asleep while the Head was addressing the school, and this would have been much less obvious to the pupils below if there had been more staff presence. Of course, it didn't help that Geoffrey also had an embarrassing accident, but this whole incident could easily have been mitigated with more staff. Please be there in force this Friday.

Thank-you!

Peregrine I. Grueson

Head Master's Speech Notes – End of Summer 2010

(wait for silence) Ex day-o gloria jew ventiss ett sap-yentis... pause... From the Lord cometh the glory of youth and of learning. Please be seated.

wait for settling down...

There is, ladies and gentlemen – long pause- sense of impending doom – a worm, yes – pause, bordering on a short silence – yes, a worm, an evil at the very heart of our community, a worm eating at the interior of our communal life here at St. Cretien's, and I for one am - stabbing gesture with finger – devastated – shouted – by what I see around me; evil, a worm of evil, looking at me here, even through your young eyes, which should be eyes, yea, of such innocence, yet which have witnessed things of such heinous wickedness, that I stand here before you – outstretch arms – more a victim of my own leadership than a Head Master of a pleasant school in leafy Sussex.

Raise head and neck, crane up to catch light from upper windows.

How I howl – *howl here* - inwardly when witness to such cruelty, and how my heart crunches when I have to send pupils home, as indeed has just happened with the seventeen boys and girls who have just been suspended. These pupils and their attitude are the woodworm and the gnawing – gesture by bring up fist and wrapping it round and round to look like a bare, crooked branch – alien evil which can make the strong wood of our community rotten and soft, weak and porous, dead – lower voice to a gravelly rasp – oblivion.

This has to be cut out, this has to be stopped. There may be some amusement at the end of a school year, but what happened here, especially to the catering staff, is an act of appalling inhumanity. Furthermore, what an awful and tragic burden it was on our Post Office, to lose Mr. Gregory for those three days, and, my God, it certainly wasn't pleasant for him being locked in there for all that time. How bloody dare you? Let me say now that at no point in the future will any postman doing his collections on St. Cretien's grounds ever again be ambushed in this manner, and forced into such a cramped space – shout this! - no matter what people say he may be. Absolute bastards, - severe pause - and I don't bandy words like that about lightly, I can tell you.

Leave plenty of time for the atmosphere to hang heavy with pupils' reflections

Well, enjoy your holidays, go away and relax, return in September refreshed and enthusiastic! Goodbye, and have an excellent summer!

allow for applause to die away

Loud-artay educat-see-onem in nomminy dominny
Praise learning in the name of the Lord.

Left side first please, in an orderly fashion. Follow the monitors, thank-you

HM

Hawthorn Towers,
The Wold

July 2010.

Dear Mr. & Mrs. Farrow,

As ever, a token of our appreciation for all your help with our boys, and especially with keeping Priam on the straight and narrow — We trust you will enjoy this particular vintage!

Cheers!

The Hardys

Printed in Great Britain
by Amazon.co.uk, Ltd.,
Marston Gate.